RUINING HER

MCKINLEY RANCH DUET, BOOK 1

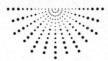

KYLIE KENT

MCCARTNEY INDUSTRIES PTY LTD

Ebook ISBN 13: 978-0-6489981-6-7

Paperback ISBN 13: 978-0-6489981-7-4

Cover illustration by
RJ CREATIVES GRAPHIC SERVICES

Editing services provided by
Kat Pagan - https://www.facebook.com/PaganProofreading

COPYRIGHT

This book contains scenes and discussions of non-consensual sexual acts, domestic violence, profanity, sexual content and violence. If any of these are triggers for you, you should consider skipping this read. This is book 1 in a 2-part duet; a cliff-hanger should be expected.

This book is dedicated to all the survivors. All who live with the internal and external scars left behind. Never stop fighting for you, never give up on finding your happy ever after.

RUINING HER - BLURB

Emily

I never thought I would be seeking shelter here of all places.

I'm out of options though. I needed a place to hide out.

Somewhere I could get my bearings and develop a plan to get myself out of the mess I've landed in.

It was a fail-proof plan. Then he found me.

I've escaped one monster, only to be captured by another.

He's determined to break me, to uncover the secrets I'm hiding. But this is one secret I can't let him discover.

Can I escape him before he ruins everything? Before he ruins me?

Josh

She was meant to stay away.

Emily, the only person in the world who's made me feel like I actually have a heart.

She made me hope that my soul wasn't as black as people say.

Hope's a dangerous bitch though, one I killed before those embers ever had a chance to flame.

Now she's back. And she's keeping secrets, ones I plan to uncover using any means necessary.

I warned her that if I ever laid eyes on her again, I'd keep her.

In keeping her, I know I'm going to do the one thing I never wanted to do.

RUIN HER.

PROLOGUE

EMILY

2010

*T*en. That's how many times I have done this in the past three years. Ten new schools. Ten new groups of friends I had to fit in with. This one is in a league of its own though. I haven't had to try to fit in to this sort of crowd before. The elite offspring of the rich and famous.

I'm sure I stand out like a sore thumb. The scholarship kid, only here because her daddy died a military hero. I hate that everyone in this cafeteria knows who I am, knows that I'm the daughter of that soldier who died.

My face was plastered all over the news six months

ago, when word broke out that my father died while saving the lives of five other men in his platoon. I should be sad. I should be missing my dad.

The thing is, I'm angry at him. Angry that he chose to save the lives of others instead of his own. Angry that he's not coming home this time. He promised me that this was going to be his last tour. I guess, in a twisted way, he didn't actually break that promise. I don't miss him though. I've grown up with him hardly ever around, so it's not a huge difference now that he's gone.

After the funeral, my mum packed up and moved us back to the Hunter Valley, a rural area just outside of Sydney. She applied for this scholarship—said it's the last time I'll have to change schools, so I might as well get into the best one there is. I'm fifteen; I have three more years of schooling left. Three years of being stuck in this gilded prison.

These rich kids know I'm not one of them. All morning I've had nothing but sneers and disgusted looks sent my way. No matter how much I paste on a smile (however fake it may be), one day, it will be real. I just have to keep pretending until it is.

I count to ten with the biggest, friendliest smile I can muster. My head high, I walk through the cafeteria looking for an empty table. Or a group willing to invite me to theirs. I don't find either.

What I do find is a table at the very back, one lone boy sitting in the middle of it. My breath halts, and my heart starts beating rapidly. This has to be the most beautiful boy I've ever seen. Golden blonde locks fall down past his eyes, complementing his tanned skin, the uniform doing nothing to hide his developing muscles.

Looking around, it's clear there is nowhere else to sit. With my head still high, and a smile so wide my face hurts, I go and sit across from the boy. The moment my tray hits the table, all sound in the cafeteria halts. I can feel eyes burning into my back, but I don't dare turn around.

Instead, I look at the boy across from me, who in turn, gives me his best scowl. A scowl I'm sure would scare off every other student here. Not me though. I am my father's daughter after all. I will not show fear.

"Hi, I'm Emily. The new girl, obviously." My voice does not give any indication of the anxiety I'm feeling from having his gaze sear through me.

"This is the part where you say hi back and tell me your name. Then, you know, we're BFFs and the rest is history. You'll be the cookie; I'll be the cream. You'll be the Tim to my Tam. You'll be the Vegemite to my toast. I think you get the drift." I stop rambling and look him directly in the eye.

There's a flicker of amusement, but just as quickly as it comes, it's gone. He tilts his head and stares at me for what seems like hours. Then, out of nowhere, he stands, picks up his milkshake and slowly, very slowly pours it over my head.

The gasp that leaves my mouth is the only indication of shock or annoyance that I'm willing to give him. My smile is plastered back on my face as I stare up at him. *I will not show him fear,* I remind myself again.

He leans down and whispers in my ear. "You'd do best to stay far away from boys like me. I'd destroy you, little girl. You're new here, so this is the one pass you get."

His cruel words and harsh tone confuse me. I know I should be scared. I should be pissed off—he just tipped milk all over me. I'm not though. I don't know what I am, but I don't want the interaction between us to stop. It's like I'm under some kind of spell.

Turning around, I straighten my back, pick up the sandwich on my plate and start eating it. I hear his heavy footsteps walk away. As much as I want to turn back and look at him, I don't.

Ten minutes later, a group of girls comes over, sits at the table with me and starts chatting away like we've always been friends. No one ever mentions the milk-shake incident. I want to ask about the boy, the beautiful, heavily disturbed boy. But for a second time today, I don't.

JOSH

2014

*J*t's the end of Senior year. Thank fucking God I'm finally getting out of this fucking soul-destroying hell they disguise as a school. The place is filled with pretentiousness on top of pretentiousness. The kids of celebrities and old money, spoilt fucking little brats. They wouldn't know a day of hard work if it hit them over the fucking head.

The one exception is *her*.

Three years and she's been the one thing I can't seem to break. It's only a matter of time though. Everyone is breakable. I take great pleasure in watching these fuckers succumb to their breaking points. I revel in their fucking tears, their pleas for mercy.

Not her, not fucking Emmy. She's a thorn in my side. No matter how much I want to break her, there's something niggling deep down that stops me from ever going too far with her. Something that makes me want to keep her in one piece. I try to ignore it, but I know it's a losing battle.

Emily. She's like an angel among the demons of hell. Her bright, sunny, happy disposition stands out like a nun in a whorehouse. It's sickening. I've tried everything to get her halo to shatter. None of my taunts or pranks have broken her.

But the thing I hate about her most is that I actually fucking like her. I've never liked anyone. Not even my own mother. I couldn't care less what happens to that woman. But Emmy, I've gone out of my way to make sure no boys here get close to her. They've tried, and they've all ended up with broken fingers or jaws.

After the first year, they got the message she was off limits. Off limits to them, and most fucking definitely off limits to me. The only thing I'd ever do is ruin her. As much as I want to do just that, I can't fucking make myself do it.

Standing in the shadows, I inhale the nicotine from between my fingers, attempting to calm the beast who wants to come out and play. I'm watching Emmy, *my* fucking Emmy, dance with some jock. A soon-to-be dead fucking jock. I heard he has scouts in a bidding war over him—he won't be any good to any footy teams with busted kneecaps.

I smile as the image plays over in my head, but it vanishes when I see the cocksucker lean in to kiss her. Fuck no, not fucking happening.

I storm up and rip him away from her. Throwing a right hook, I get him straight on his jaw; his head snaps back. He's a big fucker. I don't give him time to recover before I'm knocking his ass on the ground. I jump on top of him and land hit after hit to his head.

All I see is a red haze as the image of his lips on hers runs through my mind. I just keep striking over and over. Then I feel it, her hand on my arm, pulling me back. Her voice breaks through the fog.

"Josh, stop it. You're going to kill him," she whispers.

Blinking away the remaining haze, I stand up, grab her hand and lead her out of the ballroom. I have no idea what I'm doing. I've never dragged her off before, yet she's willingly following me.

Once I get to my Range Rover, I open the passenger door, pick her up and place her inside the car. Shutting the door gently, I run around to the other side and start driving.

Neither of us say anything. The drive is silent. I can feel her questioning gaze on me. However, she doesn't speak, not until I steer us through the ranch gates and start taking the back tracks past the bush. The ones I know lead to a little cabin in the middle of nowhere.

"You know, I should warn you. If you brought me out here to kill me, or I don't know, chop me up and feed me to pigs or something, I would have liked some warning, so I could have worn something more appropriate for the occasion."

"Pigs? Why would I feed you to pigs?" I ask her.

"Because they eat ninety-nine percent of the human body, practically don't leave a trace." She shrugs like that's a fact everyone should know.

"I'll keep that in mind."

7

I stop outside the cabin and turn the car off. "Relax, Emmy. If I wanted you dead, you would have been in the ground three years ago."

"Well, that's comforting," she replies as I'm jumping out of the car.

By the time I reach her door, she's already outside it. I don't understand this girl. Why the fuck would she follow me out to a deserted cabin? Why the fuck isn't she scared?

"Emmy, why the fuck do you trust me enough to let me bring you out to a deserted cabin in the fucking woods?" I question. I'm pissed off. Would she follow just anyone out here?

"I know you won't hurt me, Josh. You're an asshole, a little unhinged at times. But I trust that you won't hurt me." She looks me straight in the eye, momentarily sucking me into a trance.

"Come on. I want to show you something." I take her hand and lead her into the cabin. I came by earlier and hung fucking fairy lights everywhere. I had every intention of bringing her back here tonight.

"Oh my God, Josh, this is beautiful." Emmy turns in a circle, taking in the small room.

"Not nearly as beautiful as you are," I confess.

"Wait, what? You… Josh, you don't mean that." She stumbles over her words.

"I mean every word of it. Emmy, you are the most beautiful creature I've ever seen. I can't give you promises of tomorrow. What I *can* give you is tonight.

Let me give you tonight." I'm practically begging her for one night. I hold my breath, waiting for her reply.

As soon as she gives a slight nod, I slam my lips onto hers and I've finally found my home. Finally found the place where I belong. The cookie to my cream, the Tim to my Tam.

CHAPTER ONE

EMILY

PRESENT

*T*he tomato and herb aroma fills the tiny kitchen. I smile, inhaling the delicious smells. Trent is going to be pleased. Spaghetti bolognaise is his favourite; he's always happy when I cook this. I need to take one more walk through the apartment to make sure everything is orderly before he gets home.

He likes things a certain way. It's my job to make sure our home is up to scratch. I walk through the bedroom: the bed is made, the dark duvet wrinkle free, and the pillows are arranged with precision.

Next is the bathroom. I straighten the towels,

taking extra care to make sure they are folded over the rail properly and are evenly spaced. Hearing the keys in the front door, I hurry back to the kitchen.

As soon as I get there, my stomach drops. The smell of burnt sauce assaults my nostrils. No, no, no! This cannot be happening. Rushing over to the stove top, I scrape at the pan, trying to salvage what I already know I can't. I don't have time to try to cover up my error. Trent's footsteps are heavy as he makes his way down the hall.

I reach over to the knife block and pick up a small filleting blade, holding it tightly in my hand. My heart beats rapidly as I await what's coming. There's a little glimmer of hope that things will be different this time. *Hope's a fucking bitch.* The words I was told seven years ago repeat in my mind every time I start to hope for something good.

"Trent, I'm sorry. I-I… just stepped away for a moment. I can fix this," I plead.

"You just stepped away for a moment. You stupid fucking bitch! How dumb are you? How many times have I told you not to leave things cooking on the stove top!" Trent yells as he makes his way into the kitchen.

"Are you trying to burn the place down? The home I work so fucking hard for! The home I provide you!" The frying pan goes flying across the room, hitting the wall before landing on the beige carpet. I have no idea how I'm going to get the sauce stains out of the carpet.

Instinctively, I take a step, backing up to the corner

of the kitchen. I realise my mistake when it's too late. I'm trapped. I can't escape from here.

"You're so ungrateful. Is it too much to ask that dinner be properly cooked and not fucking charcoal when I get home? Huh, Emily. Why is the simplest of fucking tasks too damn hard for you?" Trent ends his sentence with a backhand across my face.

I don't dare move or make a noise. I know if I do, it will be worse. Sometimes he stops at one. Other times he doesn't. How did my life turn out like this? My dad would be rolling over in his damn grave if he knew what I was putting up with. What other options do I have though?

Trent smiles as he opens the second drawer and pulls out a wooden spoon. So, this is going to be one of the other times then. My hand grips the little knife tighter. I'm not even sure why I grabbed it. I learnt early on that it was pointless trying to stand up to Trent. He will always beat me. I've tried leaving; he's always able to find me.

I brace for the impact as I see the wooden spoon flying through the air at my face. Motherfucker, that hurts. I can't help but crunch into myself. The cry escapes my mouth as the left side of my face radiates with pain.

Trent drops the spoon, picks me up by my hair and begins to drag me out of the kitchen. I don't know what comes over me, but I start to resist. I try to escape his hold. This only makes him angrier though.

He brings his knee up into my stomach, literally

knocking the wind right out of me. I fall to the ground. "Please, stop. Trent, stop," I beg.

"If I stop now, you're never going to fucking learn your place, you stupid dumb bitch." Slap, again his hand strikes my already burning cheek.

"If you can't please me with dinner, you can please me with the only thing you're good at." Trent starts to undo his belt. He's going to rape me, again. At least it won't hurt as bad as being beat.

He lifts my dress up. I'm not allowed to wear panties. I don't even own any. Trent pushes his cock deep inside me. I scream as he enters me dry. I feel like my insides are being ripped open.

Something digs into my hand. I remember I'm still clutching the little knife I picked up earlier. Trent hasn't noticed it. I look up at him; his eyes are closed as he pumps in and out of me. Without a second thought, I bring the blade up and jam it into the side of his neck. Pulling it out again, I repeat the action before he has a chance to stop me.

Trent's eyes go wide as blood spurts out of his neck. I watch as the colour drains from his face. It feels like time stops. Maybe I did it wrong. He hasn't moved, hasn't said anything. Then his body collapses on top of mine. This is probably the moment he ends me. He's not going to take kindly to me slicing him with a knife.

After lying with his dead weight on me for a few minutes, I take the chance and try to shove him off. I roll him onto his back before getting up on my knees.

His eyes are open, his skin a pale grey colour. I'm going to be sick.

Running into the bathroom, I empty the contents of my stomach. Shit, fuck! What the fuck have I done? It's okay… it's going to be okay. He's going to wake up. I half expect him to be sitting upright when I walk back into the kitchen. He's not. He hasn't moved. There's a pool of blood around his head.

I have to get out of here. I have to leave. I wash the blood from my hands and throw on a black hoodie, a pair of jeans and my Converse. I pack the very little that's actually mine into a backpack. Heading into the bathroom, I lift the lid to the toilet cistern and retrieve the plastic bag that holds the phone and letter Josh left me to wake up to seven years ago. I've had it hiding in there all this time, only pulling the contents out to charge the battery once every couple of days, and to check if it's still connected.

So many times, I've been tempted to call the one number that is saved into the phone. I know it belongs to Josh; that is, if he hasn't changed his number since then. Seven years is a bloody long time. I don't even know why I've held onto the items for this long. I just can't seem to throw them out.

What I do know is that I need to get out of here, out of Adelaide, fast. I take the small amount of cash Trent had stashed in his bedside table. He always left it there to test me. I'd watch him count it every night. I wasn't stupid enough to ever take any of it.

I don't look at the kitchen on my way out of the

apartment that has been my home, prison and hell for the last three years. Gently closing the door behind me, I pull my cap down low, my long hair hanging like a curtain on the left side of my face. I don't need to check a mirror to know what people will see when they look at me.

It's taken me five days. I have ten dollars left to my name. But I'm here. I'm still unsure why I'm here, of all places. Why I would seek refuge in this dirty old cabin. The dirty old cabin that holds both my favourite and worst memories.

I hitchhiked with truckers from Adelaide, in South Australia, to the Hunter Valley in New South Wales. That's one thousand and six-hundred kilometres. Five days of not wanting to fall asleep, of always being on guard. I've listened intently to the radio, waiting to hear of the search that should be happening for me.

There was nothing. No mention of the murder scene I left behind, no mention of a fugitive on the run. Nothing. Trent was a cop. I know you can't just kill a cop and get away with it. I'm not that stupid. Not to mention, his brother's also a fucking cop. One that will be after me, even if it's not being publicised on the news.

Shaking the dark thoughts off, I look around the small clearing in front of the cabin. No one is here. I don't know what I expected. I knew he wouldn't be here. That's why I came; no one will be looking for me in a cabin in the woods on the McKinley Ranch. I can spend a couple of days here to regroup and come up with a game plan as to how I'm going to get myself out of this mess.

With each step I take towards the cabin, the memory of the last time I was here hits me hard. There hasn't been a day I haven't thought of that night, a day where his face hasn't made an appearance in my mind.

"What I can give you is tonight. Let me give you tonight," Josh pleads with me. I shouldn't be here. I shouldn't be anywhere alone with Josh, the boy who has tormented me, yet also protected me for the last three years.

I know he's the reason why boys stopped paying attention to me. I also know he's the reason why nobody ever gave me any kind of grief for being the poor girl at school. He has barely said two words to me since that first day in the cafeteria.

The only thing I ever get from him is a scowl and dirty looks. I've attempted to talk to him. Each time, he walks away from me like I'm a ghost, like he can't hear or see that I'm right in front of him.

The little notes that were left in my locker every day, I've always suspected they were from him. He just confirmed my suspicions when he called me Emmy; no one ever calls me Emmy. Those notes, they were all addressed to Emmy.

To have him standing in front of me now, confessing that he wants to give me tonight... My mind is telling me to run, run far and fast. This boy is psychotic. This is probably one of his sick and twisted games. I've seen the kind of stuff he's done to other students. Never me though. It was like I didn't exist—besides the occasional prank I've long suspected he's behind.

Yet, I can't help but nod, can't help but let him give me this one night. Within seconds, Josh's mouth is on mine, his smooth, full, soft lips pressing down hard onto my own. The spark I feel, the one that happens whenever I make physical contact with him, it's alight like fireworks and wreaking havoc through my body. I'm burning up.

Josh's tongue swipes against the seam of my lips; my mouth willingly opens for him. Our tongues fight against each other. Little moans sound through the room. I don't know if they're coming from me or him. I don't even care anymore. I need more. I want more.

My fingers trace along my lips as the memory of the best kiss I've ever had taunts me. I've never felt as safe as when I was in this cabin with Josh that night. Never felt more cherished, more treasured than when Josh took his time worshipping my body.

It was heaven. That night was the best night of my life. Then the morning came, and I woke up cold and alone. There was a note and a phone next to me. The same note and phone I've carried with me for seven years. I could recite the written words from memory. I knew then I would never see Josh again. I also knew then that I hated him, hated him with everything in me. I pull the scrunched-up paper from my pocket and read it again. I need the reminder of why I can't call him. Why I can't let him find me here.

. . .

Emmy,

I'm sorry it has to be this way. You need to leave town. You need to leave and never look back. This is not the place for a girl like you.

You are the first person to ever make me feel anything. But you also make me hope, and hope is a damn bitch for someone with a soul as black as mine. That's why I can't keep you.

I know I'd only ruin you, tarnish your halo until it cracked and fell down. If I ever see you again, run. Run from me. Because I promise I won't be able to give you up a second time. I won't be able to let you go.

Yours always,
Josh

P.S. Keep this phone with you always. I'm one phone call away if you need anything at all. Just know, if you do call, if you use the phone to contact me, it's the beginning of the end for us both.

I read it every time I think of caving and calling Josh for help. Deep down, I know he'd help me. I also know I'd never let him. Now is no exception. I will figure this out. I will get myself out of the mess I've created.

Just as I'm making my way to the door, I hear a woman shouting from inside the cabin. Peering through the dirty window, I see a dark-haired woman sitting against the back wall with her hands tied.

Please tell me this is not where Josh is bringing all of his women. Oh God, what if he's in there with her? She yells out "stop" and starts talking to someone about how Dean and Josh will find them. I duck down out of view and keep listening.

This girl needs help. She's obviously a friend or something of Josh's. As quietly as I can, I make my way back into the bushes and sit against a gum tree. What do I do? I can't call him. I can't let him find me. I also can't just leave that girl in there.

Pulling the phone out, I press the number I've wanted to press for so many years. The phone rings for so long I don't think he is going to answer. Then I hear his voice on the other end.

"Emmy, what's wrong?" Josh asks after a moment.

"Josh, I… I'm down at the cabin. Um… our cabin. There's a girl in there. She's in trouble, Josh. I saw through the window. I went to help her, but then she started yelling at someone named Sarah. And she… she said your name. I don't know what to do… What do I do?" I ask.

"Where are you now?" Josh's voice cracks. I can hear him start to run. Huh, maybe this girl is his girl-friend or wife, and he's really worried about her. I don't have time to analyse the way that thought makes me feel right now.

"I'm behind the cabin, in the bushes. I should go and help her, Josh. I can help her," I tell him.

"Stay hidden, Em. Do not come out of that spot until you hear me or Dean calling for you, okay?" Josh yells over the sound of an engine revving.

"Okay," I agree, although I have no plans of letting him find me. I'm just going to stay here long enough to know that he found the girl and that he can help her. Then I'm out of here. I need to look for a new place to hide out.

CHAPTER TWO

JOSH

*a*s soon as I saw Emily's name flash across my phone, my heart stopped momentarily. I've waited seven fucking years to see that name on my screen. I've never allowed myself to hope that it would happen, because hope is a fucking bitch who only ever disappoints.

Letting her go was the one selfless act I've ever done. I've never cared about anyone before her, and I haven't cared about anyone the same way since. She took my breath away every time I saw her, made me murderous every time I watched another guy flirt with her. I wanted to destroy her and protect her all at the same time. It fucked with my already fucked-up mind.

Memories of Emily hit me like flashbacks as I speed through the bush on my dirt bike, towards the cabin.

Our cabin, she called it our cabin. Like it was some secret hideaway of ours. When in all reality, it's the place I took her one time, where I worshiped her before warning her to get the fuck out of this town, my town.

She took my warning. I haven't seen or heard from her since. Until now. Of all the times she had to call, now was that time. Stopping five minutes down from where I know the cabin is, I cut the motor and signal for the rest of the guys to do the same.

"We need to walk from here. About five minutes away, down that direction..." I don't even finish my sentence before Bray starts running towards where I pointed.

Fuck! If his impulsiveness gets Ella hurt, or worse, Emmy, I will fucking kill him. The urge to maim and murder is strong right now. My skin feels like a hundred ants are crawling all over me. I need the blood. I need the destruction. There's one person who's first on my list.

Sarah, never met the fucking woman, but she's abducted Ella, my brother's new wife. That shit will not fly with me. The fact that she's a woman means nothing when she's threatening my family.

I may be a cold-hearted bastard with a black soul, but I have developed a soft spot for Ella. I don't know how, but as soon as she kneed me in the balls a week ago at Dean's house, I took to her. She makes me feel shit I'm not used to fucking feeling. It's different from the feelings Emily evokes though.

23

With Emily, it's like I'm only ever alive when in her presence. She's literally the other half of my soul, the light side, the good side. I remember when we first met, she said we would be best friends, some shit about being the Vegemite to her toast. She wasn't wrong about us being each other's match.

But she was wrong about us being best friends. I didn't have friends, and I sure as shit didn't have girl-friends. What I did have were the twisted mind games I liked to play on all the other spoilt little brats that went to our school.

I try to catch up with Bray, but that fucker is fast. I watch as he barges through the cabin door, before I hear the unmistakable sound of a gunshot. Fuck. As much as I want to look around the bush behind the cabin and find Emily, I need to make sure Ella is okay.

She has to be okay.

I wouldn't say I care deeply for my brother, but I don't hate him—which is a far cry from how I feel about every other fucker around here. I don't want him to lose Ella after just getting his shit together enough to claim her.

As I enter the cabin, I see Ella against the wall. Dean's already crouched down in front of her, untying her hands. I inspect her body from head to toe. She has dried blood on the side of her head—other than that, she looks okay.

Thank fuck. My eyes scan the room, landing on the woman currently on the floor; she's trying to crawl towards the gun only a few feet away from her.

A calmness comes over me as a smile graces my lips. *This*, I'm going to fucking enjoy. Effortlessly picking her up by her hair, I pull her so her back is against my chest. She lets out a little cry—music to my ears.

If she's seeking empathy from me, she won't find any. I'm not capable of it. My mother had me tested, and according to the experts she hired, I'm a lost cause. A textbook psychopath, no empathy, no conscience. I agreed with their findings until Emily came along and made me second guess my own level of fucked-up-ness.

I may not have empathy for anyone else, but for her, I think I do. I made sure no one ever bullied or outcast her at school. I made sure she was surrounded by friends and was accepted. Without my interference, she would have been a loner, ostracized for being the poor scholarship kid.

I force my thoughts back to the whining bitch currently in my hands. I lean in and whisper in her ear so that only she can hear me.

"I would really fucking love to take my time with you, love. But you see, I have a girl outside waiting for me. So, as much as I want to slice your skin from your body, inch by inch, and listen to your screams and pleas, I can't. I'd really fucking love to tarnish this perfect skin of yours with my knife. Unfortunately, we're both going to have to settle for me twisting your scrawny little neck though. Because, like I said, places to be, people to see. You know how it is, right?"

She doesn't get time to answer before my hands

take hold of her head and I twist. I feel the moment her neck snaps as I let her body drop at my feet. Damn that felt good.

"I'll be back to clean this mess up later. Don't fucking touch it," I tell Zac—Ella's older brother and my own brother's best friend.

Just as I'm about to walk out the door, I stop and turn around to see Ella's wide eyes. Fuck, I should have taken into account who was here. Well, she's bound to eventually find out how fucked up her new brother-in-law is anyway.

Crouching down beside her, I reach out and tuck her hair behind her ear. I expect her to pull away from my touch, to be afraid of me. She'd be wise to be afraid of me. I don't know why Dean hasn't warned her away from me yet.

"I'm really fucking glad you're okay, sweetheart," I tell her, kissing her forehead.

"Thank you. I'm really glad you're okay too," Ella replies.

I get up and walk out of the cabin, stepping over Bray, Ella's other fucking brother, who's currently on the ground with what looks like a bullet wound in his ass.

I make my way behind the cabin and call out to her. I know she's still here. I can feel her.

"Emmy, where are you?" I wait, expecting to hear her reply, or see her blonde head pop up from somewhere. All I get is the sounds of birds and the rustling of animals scurrying away from me in the bush. Even those fuckers know to steer clear of me.

"Emmy, I know you're here. I can feel you. You're better off coming out of your little hiding hole," I yell.

Still no answer. Huh, guess she really doesn't want to be found. Too bad, now that I can finally feel her presence again after seven years, I'm not about to let her go.

"I will find you, Emmy," I call out, still getting no response. I stop mid step and continue to listen.

I listen to the sounds of the foliage, the animals, the wind. I block it all out and listen closer. That's when I hear it. The tiny little sob. The sound that fucking guts me.

Why the fuck is she crying? She should never be fucking crying. I don't like this. I don't know how to deal with these fucking feelings. This is why I made her leave all those years ago. Fuck it.

I head towards where I heard the tiny sob. There, propped against a gum tree, is my Emmy. I approach slowly, sitting down in front of her. She doesn't look up.

Five minutes pass, and I'm still sitting here on the fucking ground, waiting for her to look up at me. I want to see those blue eyes of hers so fucking bad. I want to see her beautiful face. Right now, I can't see shit. She's wearing a black cap, her long blonde hair hanging like curtains around her face.

I can feel it in my gut; something is wrong. I know

it's been seven years, but this is not my Emmy. This is not the bright, bubbly girl I spent years watching over.

I reach my hand out towards her face. My stomach drops as her whole body flinches away from me. She curls her arms around her legs. I drop my hand, my fist opening and closing. I'm out of my fucking element here.

This is the girl that never shied away from me. She never let me see fear, while all those other fuckers would beg, cry and plead for mercy. Not Emmy—she was capable of going toe to toe with the devil.

Now she's shrinking away from him. From me. I don't fucking like it.

"Emmy, look at me, please." My voice is hoarse. I'm practically begging her to look up at me. The moment she does though, I wish she hadn't.

"What the fuck? Who the fuck did this, Emily? I need a name right the fuck now!" I stand up and start pacing, my hands balling into fists. I can feel the blood rushing through my veins; never has the need to kill been this strong.

I stop and stare down at her. Half of her face is green and yellow. Some fucker has used her as a damn punching bag. Seeing her like this, curled into herself, bruised and broken… I can't process it.

Taking a breath, I sit back down in front of her and grasp onto her hands. She tries to pull away. I don't let her. I will not have her fucking scared of me. She's not fucking allowed to be scared of me.

"Emmy, you know I would never do anything to hurt you." I wait for her to acknowledge me.

A slight nod of her head is all I get. That's all I need.

"I have to know if you're hurt anywhere else." I don't want to hurt her any more than she already is. I have to know what I'm dealing with here.

"I'm okay, Josh. I'm not hurt. I've had much worse. I'm sorry... I shouldn't have come here. I'm just going to go. I won't bother you again. I promise." Her voice is whisper quiet.

I tilt my head to the side and inspect her. I can't see much. She's hiding under a baggy hoodie and a pair of jeans.

"Babe, if you think I'm letting you walk away, you're crazier than I fucking am. Come on, let's go." I pull on her hands until she's standing.

Her back straightens, she picks her head up slightly, and I see a tiny glimmer of the Emmy I knew.

"I'm not going anywhere with you. I'm going..." Her sentence is cut off when I bend at the waist and throw her over my shoulder.

I'm an asshole. I should be more careful with her body in case she is hurt anywhere else. But I need to get her out of the fucking woods.

Emily starts pounding her tiny fists on my back. "Put me down, you asshole! I can bloody well walk, you know!" She gets more infuriated when I don't acknowledge her screams.

Good, show me your fight, baby. You are not some weak little girl. You're the strongest girl I fucking

29

know. I will make sure that girl comes back, no matter who I have to fucking squash to make it happen.

Placing her on my dirt bike, I jump on behind her and kickstart the engine. We are off and speeding through the woods before she knows what's happening.

⌐

STOPPING right at the back door, I jump off the bike, picking Emily up with me. She doesn't fight me; she's oddly quiet as I carry her up the stairs to my room and straight through to the bathroom. I step into the shower and press the button on the wall that makes water fall directly on top of us from the overhead rain-water showerheads.

"Ahh, what the hell, Josh?" Emily shrieks as I put her down. I hold her arms until she is steady on her feet.

"Sorry, give it a minute. It'll warm up." Reaching behind my back, I pull my shirt over my head and dump it on the floor.

I then take the cap off Emily's head, before grasping for the bottom of her hoodie. Her hands are quick to come out and halt my movements.

"Stop. What do you think you're doing?" she hisses as she steps away, coming to a standstill when her back hits the wall.

"Either you remove the jumper, or I will. It's soaked, babe. You can't stay in wet clothes."

"They wouldn't be wet if you didn't turn on the

shower. And I'm not getting naked in front of you." Her arms fold over her chest.

"You're forgetting you don't have anything I haven't already seen. Now, you can either let me help you, or you can remove that hoodie yourself. Either way, the clothes are coming off."

Emmy shakes her head no. She's forgetting who she's dealing with. People don't say no to me. But I can't be my usual asshole self with her. She's like a fragile little trapped bird at the moment, just looking for that open window to fly out.

"Emmy, I'm not going to fucking hurt you. I'm not going to touch you—well, not in any way you don't want me to. I just need to see how badly you're hurt, that's all." I don't make a move to close the gap she's put between us, even though my hands are screaming to rip her clothes to shreds already.

"I… I can't. Please, Josh, don't make me do this." Tears fall down her cheeks as she pleads with me.

I don't like her submissive pleas. It's not her. The sight of tears running down her cheeks does not sit well with me. I can usually take pleasure in others' pain and sorrow. Hers, it's different. And I don't fucking know how to deal with it.

I'm running out of patience and ideas. I have to get out of here before I do hurt her. Before I become the monster I am.

"I'll leave some clothes for you on the bed. Make no mistake, Emmy, this conversation is not over." Stepping out of the shower, I remove my wet boots and jeans before wrapping a towel around my waist. I can feel her eyes on my back the whole time.

I really need to fucking get away from this girl. I don't like people not doing what I tell them to, but I can't seem to bring myself to force her to comply either. I need to regroup. I will find out what the fuck happened to her, and when I do, someone's blood will stain my hands.

For now, I'm going to have to settle with feeding my pigs.

"Break Stuff" by Limp Bizkit screams out of the speakers. This shed is soundproof; there's no way to hear what goes on inside. To anyone looking, it's just an indoor pigpen. I've just thrown the last limb of that crazy bitch into the middle, watching as the pigs go nuts eating the human remains.

They love human meat. And I love that I can dispose of a body so easily and effortlessly. I remember thinking Emily was nuts when she thought I had a heap of pigs somewhere that I'd feed her to. It's because of her that I bought these guys as tiny piglets. I hand-raised them like they were my own children.

Leaning against the wall, I inhale the nicotine of my cigarette, watching as the smoke fills the air. I should go back into the house and check on Emily. I'm sure she's going to be pissed about the fact that I locked her in my room.

Flicking the butt of my smoke on the floor and squashing it with my boot, I turn to leave just as the door opens. Dean and Zac walk in; both men look towards the pigs and then back at me.

"You know I've done some messed up shit in my life, but this here is second-level fucking crazy, Josh," Zac says, shaking his head.

"You're welcome to leave, or better yet, be dessert," I inform him, to which, he just smirks at me. Cocky bastard.

"We're heading back into the city in the morning." Dean breaks the stare-off between me and Zac.

"Okay, tell Ella I'll meet her for breakfast at 7:30 a.m. If she's not there, I will be breaking your fucking door down."

"Sure, I'll let her know." Dean shrugs his shoulders before asking, "Are you sure you won't have your hands full? If you say you're meeting Ella, you have to be there. I won't have her disappointed if you don't show. For some strange ass reason, she likes you."

"Why wouldn't I show?" I ask.

"I don't know, Josh. How about that little blonde you have locked up in your room?" Dean knows way too much about my past with Emily. He's way too fucking intuitive when it comes to me.

"She won't be a problem. She also has a fucking name asshole—*use it*. Now, if you'll both excuse me, I have things to do." Just as I think I'm getting out of this conversation, Dean stops me with a hand on my chest. I look down at his open palm, then back up at him. But he doesn't remove it. Anyone else, I would have chopped that hand off their arm already.

"Not so fast. What are you planning on doing with Emily?" he asks.

"That's really not any of your fucking business," I growl at him.

"I know how badly she messes with your head. It's not her I'm worried about. It's you. So again, what are your plans with Emily."

"It's simple really. I'm keeping her." I shoulder barge past him on my way out the door.

CHAPTER THREE

EMILY

*T*he warm sun shines on my face. I pull the blankets up over my head to block out the light. Mmm, these blankets are soft, silky soft. Stretching out my limbs, I do a quick assessment of my body, cataloguing the various aches and pains.

The bruises on my face have become a dull ache. My ribs, a slight, sharp pain. It didn't help that Josh threw my body over his shoulder yesterday. Fuck, Josh!

I bolt upright at the memory. Looking around the luxurious room, I know it wasn't a dream. I really am in Josh's room right now. No, not just in his room... I'm in his bed.

Holding the blanket tight to my chest, I'm half expecting him to jump out of the shadows somewhere.

He's not here though. I've always been able to somehow feel him whenever he's been close.

The room smells like him; he *was* here recently. Judging by the messed-up sheets on the other side of the bed, I'm guessing he slept there. He slept right next to me—probably explains why I don't remember waking up from the usual nightmares.

I need to get out of here before he comes back, before he can stop me from leaving. The asshole locked me in here after he left me in his shower. I walked out, saw the sweatpants and shirt he placed on the bed for me, and quickly changed. It only took ten minutes of trying the door handle for me to give up on it and climb into the bed. I told myself I would just lie down for five minutes, regroup and come up with a new plan.

That's exactly what I needed now, a new plan. A plan to escape this room. A plan to fix the shitstorm that is now my life. Reluctantly, I get out of what has to be the softest bed I've ever slept in.

I can take in more of the room with the sunlight shining through the large bay windows.

The dark timber, four-poster bed sits in the middle. It's masculine (and it's very Josh), covered with dark navy bedding and black satin sheets. There's a large chest of drawers with a few little knickknacks sitting on top of it. Other than that, the room is empty. There's so much blank space it's a little eerie. Why doesn't he have more furniture in here?

There are two doors; one I know leads to the bathroom. I head for that door and freshen up as quickly as I can. I run my hands through my hair, rub some tooth-paste on my finger and pathetically try to brush my teeth.

It will have to do. I don't plan on seeing anyone anyway. I plan on sneaking out without being noticed. The only problem is I know how big this house is. I came to a house party here once. Josh's older brother, Dean, threw one when he was a senior at school. My friend Bella and I snuck in.

I had hoped to run into Josh, only he was nowhere to be found. That was basically my last years of high school—me, trying to get glimpses of Josh, while also hoping he would notice me. That he would see me.

I finally got that wish granted on graduation day. He noticed me. He cherished me, only to then abandon me and tell me to leave town. The memory both saddens and angers me. How dare he give me one night of pure bliss, of happiness like I've never known, only to shatter my world the next morning.

With renewed determination and a little anger, I storm to the door and yank on the handle. I'm expecting it to be locked again, so when it actually opens, I fall back with the force of my pull. Huh, what game is this psycho playing? I remember just how much he tormented the other kids at school. He loved playing mind games with everyone.

The hallway is clear; no one is around. The house is so silent I could mistakenly think I'm the only one here. I make my way down the winding marble staircase as quietly as I can. Once I get to the bottom, there are three different hallways, all leading in different directions. It's like a game of eeny meeny miny moe, and I have no idea which way to go.

One of these has to lead to an exit somewhere. Choosing the one to the left of the staircase, I follow the long walkway, tiptoeing past numerous closed doors. Why the hell are there so many doors in this place? How many rooms does one house need to have?

I get lost in my thoughts. By the time I realise it, I'm already in the kitchen with a pair of icy blue eyes staring back at me. My steps stop, my heart rate picks up, and an unfamiliar feeling rushes over me—a reaction to what I've walked in on.

Josh is sitting at the bench with the girl who was in the cabin. He has one arm around her, hugging her as she rests her head on his shoulder. My eyes flutter between Josh and the arm he has around another woman.

It's irrational of me to have any feelings of jealousy, yet I recognise that these feelings are just that—the kind of irrational, stupid jealousy that I have no right to feel. I don't even know Josh anymore. Then again, can I really say I ever knew him?

One night together does not count for anything. He clearly has not been hung up on me all these years. I can't help the violent thoughts running through my head, or the fact that I want to go and rip his damn arm off.

I can't remember a time I've ever been jealous

before. Actually, that's not true. I used to get crazy jealous whenever the girls at school would talk about how hot Josh was, or how much they wanted just one night with him. Thankfully, I don't think any of them ever got that one night.

However, *I did*, and even though I hate him for how it ended, it was still one of the best times of my life. I can still feel the ghost of Josh's hands all over my body. What I wouldn't do to feel that again…

"You need a cool drink or something, Emmy?" Josh's voice breaks me out of my trance.

My face heats with embarrassment at the realisation he could possibly know what I was thinking. The girl beside him sits up straighter and looks in my direction. She only just noticed I was in the room.

"No thank you. And it's Emily, not Emmy." I cross my arms over my chest, trying to cover up the fact that I'm not wearing a bra. I can feel my hardened nipples rubbing against the fabric of his shirt.

My feet are frozen to the spot, my body betraying me. Josh stands up and walks around the bench. My mind is telling me to run, run in the other direction and never look back. But my feet don't move. They don't move when Josh approaches me as he undoes the buttons on his flannel shirt and takes it off.

They don't move as he wraps that shirt around my shoulders, unfolding my arms to guide each one through the long sleeves. My feet still stay rooted to the spot when Josh leans in and whispers in my ear.

"I know what you're thinking, Emmy. I also know

your nipples are not rock-hard right now because you're cold. Unless you want me to throw you down on that bench and wrap my mouth around those delicious fucking nipples of yours right now, keep this shirt on." He straightens and takes my hand in his, leading me to the bench before sitting me on a stool.

"Emmy, this is Ella, my sister." He puts extra emphasis on the word *sister*.

I tilt my head and squint my eyes at him. Does he think I'm stupid? He doesn't have a sister. "Sister? Really? Since when did you get a sister?" I ask.

Josh smirks as one eyebrow raises. "Since a week ago, when Ella here was stupid enough to marry my brother."

"Don't be an ass, Josh. No matter what you think, it doesn't suit you," Ella directs to Josh before facing me. "I want to thank you for helping me yesterday. I'm really fucking glad you showed up when you did."

Before I know it, Ella is standing up and has her arms wrapped around me. She squeezes me in a tight hug. I wince at the sharp pain that radiates through my ribs. My body stiff, I know I should hug her back, but I'm not used to this kind of thing. I haven't had anyone hug me for so long.

Ella pulls away suddenly. "Shit, I'm so sorry. Are you okay?" she asks with what seems to be genuine concern.

"Uh, yeah, I'm good. Just slept wrong. It was really nice meeting you, Ella. Congratulations on your marriage. Uh, I should probably be going."

Just as I stand up, Josh places a cup of coffee in front of me. "Sit down. We're having breakfast." His voice is rough, commanding.

I sit back down quietly. I'm so used to taking orders I don't even argue. Anxiety rains terror through my body as I wait for the yelling to start. Surely, it won't be long. It's probably better to just get it over with.

Only, when I look up, both Ella and Josh are staring at me and no one is yelling. I can see concern on Ella's features. It makes me uncomfortable and I can't seem to meet her eyes. Josh looks angry though; that's a look I can cope with. I know what to expect from anger.

Needing to get the attention away from me (and to calm Josh's rage), I pick up the cup and take a sip. My hands shake. I don't know why he's angry. I don't know what I'm supposed to do to make him happy. At least with Trent, I knew what made him angry. I could avoid upsetting him.

The image of Trent's lifeless stare, blood pooling around his head as he lies on the kitchen floor, haunts me. I can see it even with my eyes wide open. My hands are so shaky as I try to put the cup back down on the bench, that the coffee spills over and onto the pristine white marble benchtop.

Oh no! This can't be happening. I jump up. "I'm so sorry. I'm really sorry. I-I'll clean it up. I promise. I'll get it clean. You won't even know there was a spill," I stutter out, my eyes scanning around the kitchen for where I can find cleaning supplies.

I spy the sink and head for it. "It's my fault. I should have been more careful. I'll be more careful. I promise."

Just as I make it back over to the bench, arms wrap around me from behind. I automatically bring my hands up to cover my face. My body draws in on itself. Josh spins me around, caging me in.

I can't bring myself to look up at him. My hands are still raised defensively.

"I'm going to go pack. I'll come find you before we leave." With those parting words, Ella walks out. Josh doesn't answer her. I can feel his gaze locked on me.

He grabs onto my hands and pulls them away from my face, slowly, gently, tilting my head up with his finger. My eyes connect with his. I can't read what I see staring back at me. Gone is the icy glare, and in its place, something I've only seen reflected back at me once before.

"I'll never hurt you, Emmy. I promise." Josh's voice is a whisper.

I nod my head in acknowledgement. I don't know how to answer him. Deep down in my soul, I believe he wouldn't hurt me. But my body has been accustomed to protecting itself. It's all I've known for the past three years.

"I need a name, Emmy, now." Gone is the whisper, gone is the look of devotion I saw momentarily. Back is the icy glare, the harsh tone.

I shake my head. I can't possibly tell him. He can never know what I've done. Plausible deniability. If the cops do catch up with me here, at least he has plausible deniability. He wasn't knowingly harbouring a fugitive.

"You know I'm going to find out anyway. It will save us both a lot of time if you just tell me."

"I can't, Josh. Just let me go. I'll leave and you can pretend you never saw me. Please."

Josh shakes his head. "There's only one problem with your plan, Emmy."

I'm afraid to ask, afraid to know the answer, but I question him anyway. "What?"

"I can't just forget I saw you. I haven't been able to forget about you in the past seven years. I can still taste you on my tongue. I can still feel the smoothness of you under my fingers." Josh traces his fingertips up and down my arm, leaving behind a trail of goosebumps.

I shouldn't be feeling turned on right now. I haven't been remotely interested in sex for a long time. My thighs tighten together; my body shivers. All I want to do right now is climb this man like a damn spider monkey. The thought of how quickly my body betrays my mind with just a single touch is terrifying.

"J-Josh, I..." I let my sentence drag off. I'm not sure if I'm begging him to give me the release that I so desperately want, or asking him to stop.

Josh pushes his whole body against mine. My back digs into the benchtop behind me. I can feel the hardness of his cock pressing into my stomach. I need to put a stop to this. I need to get some distance between us.

"Stop." My voice is nothing but a whisper as I push against his chest. The bastard doesn't even budge.

"Your voice is telling me to stop, but you don't really want me to stop, Emmy. Do you?" His tongue trails up the side of my neck. My head tilts, granting him better access.

Traitorous fucking body. Damn it feels good, so good. It doesn't matter how good it feels, I know it won't end with *good feelings*. It never does.

"I need you to stop, please." As soon as the words leave my mouth, my eyes widen. Panic overtakes me and I wait for the slap that's bound to come. I wait and wait. Josh stares down at me without saying anything, his jaw clenched.

He pulls my stiff body into his and wraps his arms around me, burying his face into the crook of my neck. He whispers, "I've never felt the need to maim and torture as much as I do right now. When I find out who did this to you, Emmy, there won't be a stone they can hide under. I'm going to take great pleasure in staining my hands with their blood."

Little does he know... he's never going to get that opportunity.

CHAPTER FOUR

JOSH

*H*olding Emily's stiff body tight against mine, I do my best to rein in the overwhelming anger threatening to take over. Anger is an old friend. I'm familiar with the sensation, but the level of anger I'm feeling now, it's at an all-time high.

I need to find out who did this to her. I need their blood, like I need air. I'm fucking angry that she didn't come to me sooner. How long has she been being abused? How long has some fucker been using her for a fucking punching bag?

I'm fucking furious at myself. If I hadn't been such a weak fucking coward all those years ago, this wouldn't have happened. I would have kept her. I would have protected her.

Picking her up, I carry her back to my bedroom

—*exactly where she should be*. The sight of the perfectly made-up bed stops me. I know the maids don't come in here until at least 11:00 a.m.

"Did you make the bed, Emmy?" I ask.

"Yes. Is it not how you want it? I can fix it," she says, as she tries to shimmy herself down from my body.

"It's fine. But you don't need to do that. We have maids who will come in and tidy up every day."

"I don't mind doing it. I messed it up. I should clean it," she mumbles out.

Walking through to the bathroom, I sit her on the vanity while I turn the taps on to run a bath. I'm sure I've got some bubbles or shit somewhere in here. Digging through the cabinets, I find a bottle of jasmine bubble bath. I pour a good amount in, testing the water as I strip my shirt over my head.

I can hear Emmy counting quietly behind me. When I turn around, I find her counting the finger spaces between the hanging towels. I'm at a loss for words as I watch her rearrange the towels until they are evenly spaced apart.

Emmy is so transfixed by what she's doing, she doesn't notice me come up behind her until I have my arms wrapped around her, my hand covering hers on the towel rail.

Her porcelain white skin is the polar opposite of my tanned and tarnished hand. "The towels are fine, babe. You don't need to fix anything. You could throw them all down on the floor and I wouldn't care."

I lift her hand off the towel rail and drop her arm by

her side before trailing my fingertips along her waist, slowly lifting the bottom of her shirt. My shirt. Burying my head into the crook of her neck, I gently kiss up and down.

"Wh-what are you doing?" Emmy asks softly.

"We're having a bath. And as good as you look in my clothes, you're not wearing them in the tub." I lift the shirt over her head. Before she can protest, I drag the track pants down her legs, lifting each foot out one at a time.

"Come on." Taking her hand, I lead her over to the bath. She steps in and sits down, pulling her knees up to her chest while trying her best to cover herself up.

Smirking down at her, I undo my jeans and kick them off. Stepping into the bath, I sit on the opposite side of her. The water is waist-deep, and although the tub could allow for more of a capacity, I turn the faucet off. I don't want her whole body to be covered by water.

Grabbing her ankles, I pull until her legs straighten on either side of me. I'm aching to yank her towards me, to make her wrap those thighs around me. I'm aching to be buried into her heat.

"You don't ever need to hide from me, Emmy." I pick up a loofah and squirt bodywash onto it.

"I look horrible, Josh. I'm covered in bruises. Why would you want to look at me?" she questions, as she finally raises her head to peer up at me.

"You are the most beautiful person I've ever seen. These bruises don't hinder your beauty, babe." I gently

47

run the loofah up and down each of her arms. She stares at me, silently.

"Can I ask you a question?" she prompts, her voice cautious.

"There isn't anything you can't ask me. I can't guarantee you'll like the answers, but I won't ever lie to you."

"Do you know someone else named Emmy?"

I'm not sure what I was expecting her to ask, but that was not it. I laugh. "No, I don't. Why?"

"Then why do you have my name tattooed across your heart?" Her hand reaches out, her fingertips tracing over the lettering that runs across the middle of my chest.

"I had this done the day after... the day after our senior graduation. I have your name on my heart, because you are the only person I've ever loved. You are the only person I love."

Her hand stills and she removes it from me. I want her hands back on me. I want her touching me.

"If you loved me, then why did you make me leave?" There's a tiny flame of fire in her eyes, a tiny flame of the old Emmy.

"I was saving you *from me*. I'm not normal, Emmy. I didn't want you to be dragged down by me. You were like this piece of light in my dark world. I didn't want to be the one to dim your light."

"You're right. You're not normal. But I loved you anyway. I would have happily stayed in that cabin with you forever. I never cared what other kids said about you at school. I never listened to the rumours, even if I knew they were true. Because even back then, I knew. I've known since I first laid eyes on you..." she whispers.

"What did you know?"

"That you were the Tim to my Tam, the Vegemite to my toast."

"You forgot the cookie to your cream," I remind her, a vivid memory of the first time I saw her coming to me. "Did you forget the part where I tipped a milk-shake over you? I'm not a nice person, Emmy."

"I haven't forgotten. I also haven't forgotten how no one ever picked on me at school. Or how every single boy who ever showed any interest in me would either leave school or come back banged up."

I shrug. "I did all those losers a favour. Also, they should have known better than to try to hook up with you."

I spend the next ten minutes rubbing the loofah all over her body, paying extra attention to her breasts and those pink nipples of hers that make my mouth water. Her breathing picks up; her cheeks are flushed. I can feel the twitch in her legs as she fights to close them. She's fighting the feelings. She doesn't want to be turned on.

Slowly lowering the loofah down her stomach until I reach her smooth, bare pussy, I press down harder and rub circles around her clit. Her head tips back and her lips part as her pelvis attempts to push into my hand.

Discarding the loofah, I replace it with my fingers, rolling them around her clit before dragging one down to her opening. My cock is hard as a fucking rock, aching to take the place of my finger as I slowly pump in and out of her.

Leaning over, my mouth closes around one of her hardened nipples, biting down gently as my tongue swirls around the tip. Fuck, I need to get my mind back on the game plan here. This isn't about my pleasure, or hers at the moment. As intoxicating as she is, as much as I want to watch her come apart from my touch, I want information more. I need the information only she knows.

Releasing her nipple, I kiss my way up her neck. *Slowly*. I want to stay right here, like this, forever. But forever doesn't exist. It's a concept only fools buy into.

"You want me to make you come, Emmy?" I ask as I slow my movements, her pussy trying to grind down harder onto my hand the more I pull away.

She nods her head, her long blonde locks falling back into the water.

"I need to hear the words. Do you want me to make you feel better than you ever have before?"

She picks her head up; her gaze locks with mine. "Yes." That one word, whispered out of her mouth... *That word*, I want to hear her screaming it over and over again.

"I want that too, Emmy. I want to make you come apart on my fingers, on my mouth, on my fucking

50

cock." I groan as one of her hands tentatively wraps around my cock.

"Fuck." I have to remove her hand. I can't think straight when she touches me. Now is not the time to lose focus.

"I need something from you. If you want to come, I need you to give me a name." I'm hoping she's so far gone with need, she forgets that she's keeping this secret.

She's not though, and she hasn't forgotten. She shakes her head no. "Please, Josh, I-I can't." Her hips continue to grind into my hand.

I remove my fingers. I'm out of the bath and have a towel wrapped around me before she even opens her eyes.

"What are you doing?" she asks.

"If you can't, then neither can I. Finish yourself off, Emmy." With that, I storm out of the bathroom, slamming the door behind me.

Fuck! Losing control, I punch the closest wall I find. I keep punching over and over again until I feel the tear of skin. My knuckles drip with blood. I need to get out of here. I can't be around her when I'm feeling so out of control.

Why the fuck won't she tell me? Is she trying to protect the bastard who's been hurting her? Fuck that, if she won't tell me who the fuck it is, I have other ways of finding out.

Getting dressed, I decide on a new course of action and head down to my office.

I've been sitting in this office for an hour, making call after call, scanning emails and answering the ones that are worth my time. I've been debating over whether or not to investigate Emmy's life. I've never second guessed my choices before, never cared what anyone thought. But it's different with her. I fucking hate that she brings these feelings out of me.

Deciding it's always better to seek forgiveness rather than ask permission, I put the call through (the same call I've been holding off). Sam's the one guy I know I can trust to get me the information I need. There's a reason he's my second in command. He gets shit done, no matter what the task. There is no dirty laundry he can't uncover, no deal he can't make happen.

"Boss, what's up?" Sam asks.

"I need some information."

"Sure, what do you need?" I can hear him inhale, before blowing out a puff of air.

"I thought you quit?" I really couldn't care less, but this fucker has been kicking the habit for the last five years, obviously not successfully.

"I did. Then I remembered who the fuck I work for and figured there's no point in trying to prolong my miserable fucking existence anyway," he replies.

"You know, if you weren't so useful to me, your miserable existence would have ended years ago."

"So you remind me, at least once a month. What info do you need?"

"Emmy—Emily Livingston. I want to know everything about her over the past seven years. I want to know what she ate for fucking breakfast every day. Everything," I grunt out.

"Emmy, huh? Why now?" I knew he wouldn't miss the nickname I slipped out. He's been asking about Emmy for the past five years, ever since he saw the tattooed name on my chest.

"She's back." That's about all the information I want to give him.

"If she's back, why don't you just ask her?" He talks to me as though I haven't already thought of that.

"I have." I take a breath in. "She turned up here fucking black and blue. Some fucker has been using her as a fucking punching bag. I want to know who. Yesterday!" My voice raises to a yell. I pick the coffee cup off my desk and hurl it across the room.

"Oh, shit. Man, okay. I'll get every bit of information you need. I'll help you feed those fucking pigs of yours with what we find too." The sound of a keyboard being hammered on echoes in the background. He's already on the job.

"I'm not feeding my babies that kind of scum," I say. Even my pigs are too fucking good for that fucker.

"Josh?" Sam queries.

"Yeah?"

"Are you going to be all right? You know I can be there in a matter of hours if you need."

"I'm good," I lie. I'm not fucking all right. But then again, I've never been all right, have I? I hang up before he can question me further. If I was capable of having friends, Sam would come close to what I imagine a best friend would be.

Just as I hang up, Ella and Dean walk through the door.

"Hey, we're heading off. Unless you need me to stay… I can stay longer," Ella offers. I really don't understand the girl. Why would anyone offer to stay and hang out with me?

"It's okay. I'll be heading back into the city tomorrow anyway." Walking around my desk, I wrap an arm around her shoulder, guiding her and my brother out of my office. "Let me walk you out."

"Are you sure you're okay? Wait, that's a stupid question. What are you planning on doing with your new houseguest?" She's cute when she's trying to get information out of me.

"Nothing that I can tell my little sister." I wink at her.

"Ew, gross! And we are the same age, idiot." She shrugs out of my hold.

I laugh at her reaction, which was obviously the wrong thing to do. Her arms fold over her chest. Her face hardens. She tilts her head and squints at me.

"Are you laughing at me right now, Joshua McKin-ley?" she seethes out.

Fuck, if I was anyone else, I'd probably be scared right now.

"So what if I am? What are you gonna do about it?" I taunt her.

"Oh man, trust me, you do not want to go there, Bro," Dean pipes in, stepping into Ella.

"Princess, he's not right in the head. You can't take him laughing at you seriously. He laughed at our grandfather's funeral when he was ten. Like full-on laughed his ass off when it was his turn to pay his respects to the man." Dean wraps an arm around Ella's waist, like he's trying to hold her back.

"It's okay. I won't do anything to him." Ella's voice drips with sweetness. She turns in Dean's arms. "I think I left something upstairs. I'll be right back." She starts running towards the stairs.

"Oh man, I'd be careful from here on out if I were you. She does not like being laughed at. This one time, she replaced Bray's shampoo with hair remover. The guy was bald, even his eyebrows were gone." Dean laughs.

"I'm not scared of your wife, Dean. She can bring her best." I shrug.

After a minute of waiting for Ella to return, curiosity gets the better of me and I ask, "What do you think she's doing?"

Dean shrugs. Before he can answer, the front door opens and our mother struts in, staff carting her suitcases behind her. She stops as she sees both Dean and I standing in the middle of the foyer.

"Boys, you're both here. Good." She comes up and wraps her arms around Dean, kissing him on the cheek. "I've missed you. You should come home more often, darling."

She then moves onto me, hugging me even tighter than she had Dean. "Looking handsome as ever, Joshua." She steps back and smiles at us.

Dean and I share a look. Who is this woman and what the fuck has she done with our mother?

Laughter from behind me causes me to turn around. "Fuck no!" I say as I pull my shirt over my head, stomping towards Ella and Emily, who are currently walking towards us in bikinis. Where did those strips of fabric even come from?

Ella stands in front of Emily with her hands on her hips. "Stop right there! I'm going to show Emily here where the pool is." She looks over at Dean.

"Babe, you don't mind if we stay for an extra hour, do you?" she asks him.

"Ah, sure, whatever you want, Ella." The pussy-whipped fucker gives in to her every time.

"Dean, tell your wife if she wants to keep all of that pretty hair on her head, then she had better move out of my way." I hear my mother's gasp from behind me. I forgot she was even there for a moment.

"Wife?" Her head moves between Dean and Ella. I'm expecting Oscar-level dramatics any minute now, except, that's not what happens.

Mum walks over to Ella and pulls her into her arms. "Dean, I can't believe you got married and didn't tell me." She steps back and cups Ella's face. "Welcome to the family, sweetheart."

"Thank you, Mrs. McKinley. But it's not completely Dean's fault. It was quick. We didn't have a wedding, just signed the papers," Ella rambles.

"Ella, you can call me Julie. Don't you worry. I'll make sure you get a wedding fit for a princess."

She turns to me. "Joshua, put your shirt back on. You're distracting the staff." She makes a point to nod her head at the two young maids who are standing at the other end of the foyer with their mouths gaping.

Emily looks their way and glares. Huh? Well, that's interesting.

"Wait, why are these girls allowed to strut around without clothes on, but I can't?" I ask like a sulking child.

"They're not naked. They're going swimming," my mother, or the woman who has taken over my mother's body, answers.

"Ella, hunny, go ahead and take Emmy to the pool. I'll have some drinks and snacks brought out to the two of you."

Once Ella and Emmy are out of the room, my mother spins on my brother and me. Pointing a finger at Dean, she says, "I'll deal with you later."

"Now you," she directs at me. "For the love of God, please tell me that girl is here of her own free will, Joshua."

I raise my eyebrows at her question. "Of course she is." It's not a complete lie; she did come here of her own free will. However, am I prepared to let her leave? Fuck no.

"What happened to her?"

"I don't know. I'm trying to find out. She turned up here like that, Mum. I didn't fucking do that." I'm not sure why I feel the need to defend myself.

"I know you wouldn't hurt her, Josh. She's probably the only person on this godforsaken Earth who you wouldn't hurt." She pauses before asking, "Are you okay?"

Why the fuck is everyone asking me that? Like I'm going to fall apart or something.

"I'm fine. But are *you* okay? Are you dying?" It's the only conclusion for her sudden motherly attitude I can come up with.

"Never been better. I'm not dying. Is it so wrong for a mother to be concerned for her sons' wellbeing?"

"For mothers, no. For you, yes," I reply.

"Well, things are changing. I have daughters. I'm sure grandbabies aren't too far off."

"Ah, you have one daughter-*in-law*. Not plural. And let's hope those grandbabies look like fucking Ella and not this ugly ass." I look at Dean.

"Don't hold your breath for grandbabies anytime soon, Mum. I just got Ella to myself. I'm not ready to share her with anyone else yet." Dean's staring in the direction of where Ella just left, like he can see through the fucking walls to her.

"Okay, well, I have a wedding to plan. I'll catch up with you boys later." Our mother walks out of the room, already clicking away on her phone.

I look at Dean. "What the fuck was that?" I ask him.

I know I'm not the best at social situations, or emotions, but that shit was fucking weird as hell.

"No idea, man. But I'm going to go drag Ella out of here before we get stuck planning the wedding of the fucking century." He storms off towards the pool.

CHAPTER FIVE

EMILY

*F*loating around in the pool, I feel free. Weightless. At peace. It's quiet in here. Dean came and dragged Ella out, saying something about escaping his mother's wedding planning before it was too late.

I like Ella. In another life, another time, I think I could have been good friends with someone like her. My life isn't destined for that. I'm not destined for the happily ever after. The sombre reality crashes over me, reminding me not to get too comfortable here. I need to plan my escape. I need to get out of here before I get Josh and his family in any trouble.

How my face isn't spread all over the news and on every paper out there, I don't know. I killed someone. Granted he deserved it, but he was still a living, breathing person and I killed him. The thing that's messing with my mind is the fact that I don't regret it. That realisation scares me. I should feel bad.

The nightmares come—maybe that's my subconscious telling me I did something I should feel bad about. In my nightmares though, I don't kill him. In my nightmares, he's still alive and he's coming for me.

What if I didn't kill him? No, I saw all the blood, the lifeless eyes. He was definitely dead. He has to be. I can handle going to jail for the rest of my life if it means never having to face him again.

A huge splash draws me out of my internal battle. I right my body, looking around for what could have made the splash. I can see the ripples in the water, but that's it. Nothing else. Surely if there was someone else in here, they would have to come up for air by now. Right?

The water stills and nothing and no one has popped up. I'm starting to get freaked out, standing here like a sitting duck. I head for the steps to get out of the pool when something grabs around my ankle and pulls me down, my scream silenced by the water. I kick out at the person holding me under. It's no use. Whoever it is wraps their arms around me and shoots both of our bodies up.

My lungs heave as I wipe the water from my face and swipe my hair off my forehead. Opening my eyes, I'm met with a sight that momentarily stops my heart.

Josh is smiling, a big beaming smile; even his damn eyes are twinkling. For a moment, a small moment, I forget that I'm mad at him, that I hate him. I get lost in those blue eyes of his. Then I remember I hate him.

Punching him on his chest while trying to wiggle myself out of his vice-like hold, I yell at him, "What the hell are you smiling about, asshole?"

"What's not to smile about? I've got the most beautiful woman in the fucking world in my arms—and she's all *wet*." His voice is deep and husky.

"Does that line work on all the girls, Josh? Because if it does, you need to up your standards," I bite back at him.

"There are no other girls, babe. There is only you. There will only ever be you." He's so convincing with his words, I almost believe him. I almost want to believe him.

"Sure, whatever you say. Now, remove your hands from me before I scream bloody murder," I threaten.

Josh immediately removes his hands but doesn't move away from me. I take a step backwards myself, only to have him follow.

"You know, it wasn't that long ago you were begging for my hands to be on you, *in* you." He smirks.

"I had a momentary lapse in judgement. Don't flatter yourself. I ended up doing a better job myself."

I'm not sure where the courage to talk back to him like this is coming from. Why am I pushing him? Trying to get him to break? Get him to show me his true colours sooner rather than later? I'm waiting for him to snap and lash out at me. It's bound to happen, eventually. The longer I stay here, the more chance I have of being *that* girl again.

The one who lets a guy dictate her every move, the one who lets the guy use and abuse her to relieve his own frustration. I've decided I don't want to be that girl again. I never wanted to be her in the first place.

"You can push me as much as you like. Talk back to me with as much fight as you've got to give. There is nothing, and I mean *nothing*, you can do that will ever make me hurt you, Emmy. I may be a monster, but I'm not that kind of fucking monster," Josh says fiercely.

"You don't get it, Josh! All these bruises, all these scars. Yeah, they hurt. Yes, I've been beaten over and over again. But no amount of physical pain has ever amounted to the ache you caused when I woke up in that damn cabin alone!" I scream, and tears start running down my face. I didn't mean to tell him… I didn't want him to know how much he has the power to hurt me. *Had.* He had the power to hurt me. I won't let any man hurt me again.

Josh reaches his hand up to my face. I automatically flinch, turning my head. I feel my body go stiff, waiting for the sting. I don't feel it though; what I do feel is Josh's thumb wiping away the tears from my cheek.

"I wish you would give me a name, Emmy," Josh whispers.

I shake my head no. I can't let him know what I've done. I just need to get out of here.

"It's okay. You don't have to tell me. I'll find out anyway."

"You need to stop looking, Josh. You need to let me leave. I can't be here. I shouldn't be here."

"*Here* is exactly where you're meant to be. Here is where you belong. You can't leave, Emmy. You can't leave. You can't. Please just let me keep you for a little longer." Josh sounds almost desperate. His arms wrap back around my body as I let myself embrace his touch. I rest my head on his chest, right over where my name is printed on him.

I know I shouldn't give him reassurance, make promises I can't keep, but I do anyway. "Okay." The one word leaves my mouth, sealing my fate, his fate, our fate.

What will he do when he finds me gone? Because as soon as I get the chance, I will be leaving. No matter how much I want to stay right here in his arms, I know I can't.

I SPENT the rest of the day with my hand firmly gripped in Josh's as he gave me a tour of the farm. He introduced me to some of the staff, informing them I'd be staying for a while. I plastered on a fake smile and let myself believe the lie, the dream, for a little while.

This has been one of the best days I've ever had. I can almost picture a life here with Josh. Every time I let myself see a glimpse of what that might look like, a vision of dead eyes and a pool of blood overtakes my

RUINING HER

mind. I'm never going to have the fairy tale Josh is selling me.

I'm now wandering around Josh's room. He said he had some things to take care of, that he'd be in his office if I needed him. There's not much in here to look at. His closet is neat, too neat. All his clothes are perfectly hung and ordered by colour, his shoes lined up and again ordered by colour. I wonder if he does this himself, or if his maids do it for him.

Irrational jealousy overcomes me at the thought of other females doing anything for him. It should be me. I should be doing it all. No... no, I should not. What I should be doing is figuring out how to get out of this damn palace, because let's call it for what it is. This place is not a home; it's a damn museum.

I'm bored. I could wander out of the room. I know he didn't lock the door this time. But I'm so exhausted from all the walking around we did today. I decide to lie down. I figure a little nap won't hurt. Maybe Josh will come back in soon and I can talk him into taking me into the city.

$\triangledown$

"D*ID you really think you could get away from me? You fucking whore!" he yells.*

I shake my head no. "It was an accident. I-I didn't mean to. I'm sorry," I cry as I step backwards until I hit the wall. How did he find me? He's supposed to be dead; he can't be here. This can't be real.

65

But as his hand wraps around my throat, it's real. I feel it. I feel the burn in my lungs as they fight for air. He lets go, only to slap me across the face. I fall to the ground and curl up in a fetal position.

"No!" I scream out. "Stop, please. I didn't mean to!" I'm sobbing. I look up to him standing over me, his big, heavy, black boot lifted above my head and ready to come straight down. I scream as the boot starts making its descent towards my face.

Jolting upright, I look ahead, dazed. Where am I? It was just another dream. It's okay. I'm okay.

"Emmy!" Josh yells as he crashes through the door, holding a handgun out in front of him. His gaze searches every corner of the room before landing back on me. He lowers the gun and walks over to the bed.

"Are you okay?" he asks.

"I'm… I'm sorry." My voice is hoarse. I must have been screaming from my nightmare.

"Are you hurt?"

I shake my head no. I can't even tell him what happened. How can I tell him I had a nightmare about the guy I killed coming back for me? Josh places the gun on the nightstand beside the bed.

I could end everything with that gun. I could stop it all. The nightmares, these confusing feelings I'm having for Josh, all of it could be gone in just one press of that trigger.

Josh's hand grips my chin, turning my face towards him. "Get those disturbing thoughts out of your fucking head right the fuck now, Emmy!"

My eyes open wide. How the hell does he know what I'm thinking? There's no way he can know what just went through my mind.

"I won't let anyone fucking hurt you ever again. Even yourself," he vows.

"I-I..." My mouth shuts. What can I tell him?

"What did you dream about?" he questions.

"I don't remember." The lie slips out way too easy.

"You're lying. But that's okay, because whatever monster you see in your dreams, Emily, I can promise you... that monster has nothing on the darkness of my soul, of the monster within me, or the kinds of things I plan to do with *him* as soon as I find out who he is."

"Your soul isn't dark, Josh. I've seen it." I have no idea why he thinks he's such a monster. Sure, he's a little unhinged at times. But the way he is with me, the way he's always been, I know he loves me in his own messed up way.

If only love were enough to change things... If only love could fix this mess I've put myself in...

"You're probably the only person other than my mother that sees any good in me, Emmy." Josh stands up, tipping his boots off before pulling his shirt over his head. I get so lost in all that is Josh. Big, tanned, broad shoulders. Wide chest, abs that lead into a V right down his waistline. My eyes travel back up his body. His blonde hair falls onto his forehead, covering those blue eyes a little.

"Move over, Em," he orders as he pulls the blankets back.

"What are you doing?" I ask stupidly. I can clearly see he's getting into bed.

"I'm getting into bed," he says.

"But why here? Surely there are a million other beds in this palace?" I ask him.

He tilts his head and stares at me. "Emmy, this is my bed. I'm not sleeping anywhere else."

Shit, I didn't think of that. I go to get up. "I'm sorry. I can go into another room. Or leave, or, or… I don't know," I offer.

"Emmy, move over. We've already discussed this. You are not leaving. If you try to move to a different bed, I'll just follow you anyway. Save us both the loss of sleep and just shove over a little already."

I scoot to the other side. "Just so you know, this does not mean I like you. In fact, we should draw a line down the middle of the bed if we have to share."

Josh laughs, the sound unfamiliar. I'm not sure how often he ever laughs, but I know it's not often enough. "Babe, I had my fingers buried inside your pussy this morning. Not to mention, I've had my cock buried inside that pussy of yours. Even if it has been way too fucking long since, he's been there and plans on being there again."

"Thanks for reminding me just why I hate you! And that cock of yours won't be getting anywhere near me again." I huff as I start lining pillows down the middle of the bed.

"You don't hate me, Emmy. You only wish you could. You can't hate someone you love. Trust me, I've tried to hate you for years, thinking it would make things easier. I've hated you for the way you make me feel. I've hated you for making me want a different future. I've hated you for making me want a future at all. But even with all that, the love I feel for you outweighs all the hate even I could muster up," he says this as he throws the pillows I just laid out onto the floor.

"Yeah, well, I've hated you just as much. So, you hold on to that hate; it will save both of us in the end."

"Don't you know, Emmy?" he asks.

"Know what?"

"There is no end to us. There will *never be* an end to us," he says as he lies down, pulling me into his arms.

I hate that he makes this feel good. And I hate myself more for wanting this to last longer.

CHAPTER SIX

JOSH

*T*he phone on my bedside table is blaring. Reaching a hand out, I pick it up before bringing the receiver to my ear.

"What?" I ask.

"Joshua, that's no way to answer the phone," my mother's voice chastises through the line.

"It's also not polite to call people at ungodly hours, Mother. Is there a reason you're calling me so early?" I ask.

"Well, I was just having breakfast with Emily and I thought you might like to join us," she sings.

At the mention of Emily, I bolt up straight and look to the empty spot on the bed, the spot where Emily should be.

"I'll be right down." I hang up. Throwing on a pair

of grey sweats, I forgo the shirt. The first thought in my head is that she's trying to leave. Even though she told me she wouldn't, I didn't believe her for a fucking second.

I can read it all over her face. She's running from something, someone. I can't let her leave. I'm afraid if I do, I'm never going to see her again. Over the last two days, I've come to terms with the fact that I don't want to live without her anymore. I never should have pushed her away in the first place. It's true what they say: *hindsight's a fucking bitch*.

On my way downstairs, I check my messages—nothing from Sam. What the fuck is taking him so long? He usually gets me the intel I need within hours. Shoving my phone back into my pocket, I reach the kitchen to find my mother at the counter. The sight is odd. She never sits at the breakfast bench, always having her meals served in the dining room.

Looking around, I note that Emmy is nowhere in sight. "Where's Emily?" I ask, heading for the coffee pot.

Pouring a glass of black coffee, I gulp a mouthful down before turning and raising an eyebrow at my mother, who still hasn't answered my damn question.

"She went out to see the stables. She wanted to see the horses."

Fuck! She's gone outside. She's probably halfway to Timbuctoo by now. I slam my cup down. "How long ago did she go out there?" I growl at my mother.

"Joshua, calm the fuck down. You are not going out

71

there to go all caveman on that poor girl. Don't you think she's been through enough? She doesn't need another man trapping her." My mother's words halt me. One, because I've never heard her cuss before, ever! And two, because she's right. I can't be another man caging Emily in. But I'll be damned if I'm ever going to let her go either.

"What do you know about what she's been through?" I ask. Maybe Emmy confided in her about what happened.

"She hasn't told me anything, Josh. And if she did, I certainly wouldn't be breaking her confidence and telling you."

"You are dying, aren't you? What is this? Some new kind of sick and twisted game? Playing the nice mother who actually gives a fuck?" My words are harsh, however true they are.

"I know I haven't been the best mother. But I'm going to be now. I'm sober, have been for six months. And the reason I know what Emmy's been through is because I've lived it. My whole marriage was one of control and abuse. I protected you boys from ever seeing it. I didn't want you to know. Your father was a smart, smart man; he never left marks where others would see them. Never lost his temper in front of anyone."

She looks down at the ground. I want to scream at her that she did a shitty fucking job of protecting us. Because my father was a cruel son of a bitch to both

Dean and me. He was worse to me—the man wanted to break me more than I was already broken.

He should have read the books my mother used to read, the ones on raising a child with psychopathic tendencies. I can't tell her any of that though—it won't do us any good.

I wrap my arms around my mum, the feeling foreign. But I don't know what else to do to help her. There's a tiny bit of me that doesn't like seeing her sad, a very tiny bit.

"I'm sorry he didn't die sooner," I say.

"So am I," she confirms as she pulls away. "Now, how are we going to get Emily around to the idea of being the next Mrs. McKinley, because I'm not getting any younger and I want grandchildren."

"Ah, I'm not... I don't... She's not leaving. I don't care what I have to do. I can't lose her again," I admit.

"I know. Go out there and take her riding. You know she was on the equestrian team in school, right?" The fact that my mother knows this surprises me.

"Of course, I know. She was on every bloody team," I say as I make my way out of the house.

$\smallsmile$

STANDING in the shadows of the stables, I remain quiet as I observe Emily interact with Jasper. A white Quarter horse with a soul as pure as hers. She looks at peace, talking to Jasper and brushing him down.

I smile at the sight of her in a pair of my track pants

and my shirt. I really do need to get her some of her own clothes, but the possessive ass that I am just wants to see her in mine.

I want to mark her, to make sure every fucker knows she's mine and only mine. I get so lost in taking her in, I don't notice the stable hand enter the building until he's approaching her.

I watch as he looks her up and down, licking his lips like he's about to eat a delicious meal. He's about to *be* the fucking meal if he doesn't avert his eyes elsewhere.

The fucker has a death wish. And I'm the goddamn genie who's going to grant it. I stay hidden in the shadows; neither of them knows that I'm here. As soon as Emmy notices she's not alone, she glances towards both exits. Smart girl. She's already looking for a way to escape a possible threat.

The fact that she even has to think like that is fucked up. She should feel safe in her own home. That's exactly the way I plan to make her feel.

"Hey there, darlin'. You need a hand?" the dead guy walking asks her.

"Ah, no. Thank you. I'm fine." Emmy's voice is quiet.

"Yes, you sure are," the cocksucker says as he rakes his eyes down her body again.

I watch as Emmy folds into her own body. Her head hangs low, her blonde hair falling (as it so often does) in curtains around her face.

"Ah, you should go. I'm meeting someone. He should be here any minute now." Emmy looks to the entrance, almost like she's praying someone else walks in.

Pulling my phone out, I type a quick text to Paul, my head of security.

Me: Clean up in the stables

His reply comes in quick, my phone vibrating in my hand.

Paul: Really, Josh? It's eight a.m. What the fuck could you have possibly gotten up to already?

Me: It's what I'm about to do that's going to need cleaning up.

Putting my phone back into my pocket, I make my way towards Jasper's stable, where that fucker is blocking the entrance and trapping my Emmy in.

"I don't see anyone else around, darlin'. It's just you and me out here. No one comes by these parts for at least another few hours." He takes a step towards her; she steps back.

Jasper starts to get agitated. Emily tries to soothe him, patting his neck. She whispers something to Jasper. And I swear I see the horse nod in agreement with her. Fuck, I must be getting crazier by the fucking day.

Emily notices me standing behind the fucker, and her eyes widen. I bring my finger to my lips, telling her to keep quiet. Pulling the knife from the ankle of my left leg, I snap my hand around him, placing the blade firmly at the base of his throat.

"I'm pretty sure the lady asked you to leave her alone," I say.

"What? No, we were just talking, that's all. I was just on my way out," he tries.

"Really? Is that true, Emmy? You wanted to talk to this guy?" I look at her, but she's transfixed on the knife I'm holding at the guy's throat. She slightly shakes her head no.

"That's what I thought. You see, this here is my girl-friend, and I don't take kindly to anyone that tries to fuck with her," I growl. As much as I want to slit his throat here and now, I don't want Emmy to see me like that. I don't want her to see how truly dark I am inside.

"I never have been one to play well with others. But Emmy here, she's a fucking saint. Always thinking of others before herself. Even though she knows you had all horrible intentions, she still doesn't want me to hurt you."

Emmy's eyes widen, before she looks down.

"The thing is, I'm going to enjoy hurting you. And I've got some hungry fucking pigs to feed."

Paul comes running into the stables, three men behind him, all four with their guns drawn. Emily gasps as she takes in the four hulking men pointing their weapons in our direction.

"Put the fucking guns away," I growl at them, not once taking my eyes off Emily. She's backed herself right up against the far wall.

Paul comes up behind me, tapping me on the shoulder. "Boss, I'll take it from here."

Like fuck he will. This fucker had every intention of messing with Emily. I'm going to make sure my face is the last thing he sees. Then he'll know to run when I meet him in hell.

"Josh, let me take him to the shed. You need to get your girl inside." Paul steps in front of me, holding his hand out.

"Fine, but nobody touches him until I get there," I demand.

"Sure, boss."

Removing the knife, I'm pleased to see the tiny speckles of blood on it, before I hand it over to Paul. One of the other guys comes up behind the fucker and cuffs his hands along his back.

Stepping aside, I wait until they're all out of the building before I make my way across to Emily, who is still up against the back wall. Jasper keeps one eye on me. I wouldn't put it past him to kick me in the back.

Emily doesn't move. Her body is still—apart from the slight tremble I can see. As soon as I get close enough to her, my hand wraps around her throat and my mouth slams down on hers.

Her lips part a little and I take the opportunity to slide my tongue inside, swiping and swirling it all around her mouth. She's rigid for a minute. I don't give up on my assault of her mouth. She tastes fucking delicious, and it just now occurs to me that this is the first time I've actually kissed her since she's returned.

Why the fuck haven't we been joined at the lips for the past two days? Because I'm a fucking idiot. This right here, this is my heaven. Pressing into her more, while my hand tightens a little around her throat, I groan as I devour her. She's giving back too. Her hands no longer attempt to push me away—no, those tiny hands are pulling me closer.

I trail my fingertips down her body. Picking her up, I wait as she wraps her legs around my waist. I need to get out of here before Jasper decides he wants to keep her.

Spinning on my heel, I'm met with Jasper's glare. The horse obviously doesn't like me as much as he likes her. Then again, who would?

Walking down the stalls, I find an empty one that looks like it hasn't been occupied for a while. I slam her against the wall, probably a little too roughly. But fuck, I'm losing my goddamn mind here.

Her little moans tell me she doesn't mind, her centre grinding up and down on my rock-hard cock. Clothes, why are we still wearing clothes? Unwrapping her legs from my waist, I hold her until her feet are steady. As I break away from her mouth, her eyes open, her gaze searing right through my soul.

"Do you trust me, Emmy?" I ask. I need her to say yes. I need her to trust me for what I'm about to do to her.

"Yes," she whispers out softly.

That one yes is everything to me. "Good, because you're going to really need to hold on to that trust right now."

CHAPTER SEVEN

EMILY

*D*id I really just say that I trusted him? I didn't even think about it before the word "yes" slipped out. It's not true, is it? I don't trust anyone. Yet, here I am, pushed up against the wall of a damn horse stable, letting Josh tie my hands above my head.

Shit. Wait! I pull on my wrists, but they're bound tight with rope. How did he manage to do that without me noticing? I was so lost in the pleasure-induced fog he keeps putting me under, I wasn't paying attention to what he was doing.

"Ah, Josh?" I question.

"Trust, Emmy," is the only thing he says before his lips fuse with mine. His taste is intoxicating. I can't get enough of it. As his tongue slips into my mouth, I suck and nibble on it. I want more. I want everything.

No, I don't want this. How could I possibly want this? What does that make me? I'm so confused. Even as I drown in all that is Josh, my mind questions my every move. I want to let go. I want to let go and escape just for a little bit. I want my mind to just stop.

"Make it stop, please," I beg quietly. I don't intend for Josh to hear my pleas. When he pulls away from me, holding my chin in his hand, he keeps our eyes locked on each other.

"Make what stop, Emmy?" his husky voice asks.

I close my eyes as I answer. I can't bring myself to look at him—he's already making me more vulnerable than I'm used to. "My mind, I want it to stop. I want to escape."

When I open my eyes, I'm greeted with Josh's smirk, his own eyes sparkling. "That I can do. Hold on," he says as he drops to his knees in front of me.

Hold on? I'm literally tied to the damn wall. What am I meant to hold on to? Josh pulls my sweatpants down, discarding them out of the way. Kneeling, he reaches up to the collar of my shirt before tearing it in half.

He sits back on his heels and stares up at me. "This is the best fucking view I've ever seen."

Picking up my left leg, he trails his lips over my calf, biting down on the tender skin behind my knee before continuing to drag his tongue along my thigh. It's a slow torture. By the time he reaches my aching centre,

I'm dripping—literally dripping—juices down my inner thighs.

Josh's tongue licks all around the lips of my pussy, without touching the spot I want him most. My hands pull on the rope, while the skin on my wrists burn with each tug.

"Please," I beg. Before I even finish the word, Josh's mouth covers my mound, his tongue licking from bottom to top. Holy fucking hell. This, yes, this is what I need.

Josh picks up both of my legs, positioning them on his shoulders. His hands are over my waist, pinning my back to the wall. The grunts and groans coming out of him are on a whole other level. He's like a starving man, someone who just found a waterhole after being lost in the desert.

His tongue swirls around my clit before trailing down and pushing into my slick entrance, pumping in and out a couple of times. He continues this pattern, travelling up to my clit before sinking back inside of me.

I'm losing my damn mind. My body is tight; my muscles become rigid. I can feel a sheen of sweat covering me, the cold breeze creating goosebumps all over my skin.

If my hands were not tied, they'd be buried in those blonde locks, holding his head to me. My hips grind into his face mercilessly. I'm chasing a release I haven't felt in years. I don't think anyone other than Josh has ever been able to make me feel this good.

My head tips back, his name leaving my lips as my thighs tighten around his head. The orgasm washes over me, and I feel it. I embrace it. The sense of pure bliss, nothing but pleasure.

Josh abruptly removes my legs, placing my feet back on the ground as he stands up. Tugging his sweats down a little, he pulls out his rock-hard cock. I don't get time to admire the view. His mouth is back on mine, the taste of my release on his tongue. It makes me hungry for him all over again.

I can still feel my core convulsing with aftershocks. Josh picks me up, my legs automatically wrapping around his waist. I moan at the feel of his smooth cock as he rubs the tip over my clit before lining himself up with my entrance.

He just holds it there, pulling his face away from mine. I open my eyes to see him staring down at me. What the fuck is he waiting for? Oh God, I swear if he leaves me hanging again, I'll… Okay, I don't know what I'll do, but it will be messy—*that* I can guarantee.

"Josh?" I ask

"I want to see your eyes, Emmy. I want your eyes open when I finally get to slide my cock into you again."

That's it? He wants my eyes open? Well, my eyes are open. I decide to take over. I'm not waiting any longer. I arch my back off the wall, tighten my legs around his waist and sink myself onto his cock.

"Fuck!" Josh grunts out.

He's so big, stretching my walls out. The slight sting

I feel stops me once his cock is fully inside me. Josh's forehead falls onto mine as he slowly pulls out before sliding back in.

"You feel so fucking good, Emmy! I thought I had made it up," he says.

"Made what up?"

"How fucking perfect you are! How this pussy of yours was made for me. You are mine!" He grunts as he starts to pick up his pace.

"Say it!" he growls.

"Say what?" I ask.

"That you're mine, that you're not leaving again. Say it!" he demands.

I can't say that. Instead, I tell him the one thing I can say, the one thing I want more than anything right now.

"Fuck me, Josh. I want you to fuck me harder." I bury my head in his neck and bite down.

Josh really picks up his pace then. He drives into me, his fingers pinching into the skin on my hips so tight... it's almost like he's afraid I'm going to disappear into thin air if he doesn't hold on. I'm going to have bruises from his fingertips after this.

Those marks, I will wear gladly. Neither of us are quiet as pleasure overtakes us. I wouldn't be surprised if the whole farm could hear me screaming right now. I can't seem to care though; all I care about right now is how Josh is making me feel. How close I am to tipping over the edge again.

"I need... Oh God, that, yes, keep doing that!" I cry

out as Josh somehow manages to angle my hips, his pelvis grinding against my clit.

Within seconds of this new position, I'm coming undone. My pussy clenches his cock, not letting him pull back out. My whole body quakes. Josh grunts as he comes, the warm liquid coating my walls.

We stand there, our chests heaving. After a moment, reality comes crashing into me. I just gave myself to the devil, the same one I swore I'd never play with again. The same one I dreamt about playing with, over and over again for the past seven years.

Fuck! I wiggle around as Josh's hold tightens under my ass. I need to get out of here, before I get myself in any more trouble than I'm already in. Getting caught in Josh's world is most certainly a recipe for disaster for me.

Josh finally slips his cock out of me and lets me stand. I don't know how I thought I was going to get away, considering my hands are still bound by rope above my head.

"Josh, you need to untie me now!" My panicked voice raises.

"No," he says as he takes a step back.

"What? What do you mean *no*? Untie me the fuck now, Joshua. This isn't funny!" I scream at him. Internally, I'm chastising myself. I know better than to scream and make demands—that only ends up with me covered in cuts and bruises.

"No, it's not funny. But do you know what *is* fucking funny, Emmy?"

"What?" I'm so angry right now. I'm literally tied up to a wall, with nothing but tattered material that used to be a shirt.

"It's fucking funny that you think you *can't* yell at me. Yell at me all you want, sweetheart. I can take your anger. In fact, your fire only turns me on. I don't remember you having that at school. You were always the people pleaser, always had a smile plastered on your face no matter what anyone said." He steps forward again, bending so his face is level with mine.

"But it's fucking hilarious that you think you're going to run out of here. It's fucking funny that you think there is a single fibre of my being that will ever let you leave. You're not leaving, Emmy. I don't care if I have to keep you tied to my bed for the rest of our lives. You are not leaving!" By the end of his tirade, he's pacing up and down the small space of the stable, pulling at his hair.

I've seen this Josh many times. He doesn't know that I've seen him. I always stayed out of sight when he would lose his shit at school. I know all the other kids were afraid of him. Not me though. I was drawn to him. I wanted to help him, just like now.

Everything in me wants to reassure him that I'm not going anywhere. That I'll stay here. However, if I say any of that, I'm more afraid I'll start to believe it myself. Because more than anything, I want the future he thinks we're going to have.

He stops pacing and stares at me, a lost look in his eyes. "Josh, you can't keep me locked away. This should never have happened. I should never have come here." I turn my head, not able to maintain eye contact with him. That expression on his face breaks my damn heart.

"But you did. You did come here. Why? Why'd you come back, Emmy?" His voice sounds pained. This is my fault. It's always my fault.

"I-I didn't know where else to go," I admit. When I left that apartment, the first place I thought of going was the cabin. It's all I thought about while hitchhiking with truckers across the country to get here.

"Why? What are you running from? What are you afraid of?" He's never going to stop asking, and I'm never going to be able to tell him.

I shake my head no. "I can't tell you. I can't. It's better for everyone if you don't know. It's better for everyone if you just let me go, Josh."

"You can tell me—all you have to do is open that damn pretty mouth of yours and talk. You won't tell me. There's a difference between *can't* and *won't*. But don't worry, I'll uncover all of your secrets, Emmy. And when I do, I have a feeling that hell is going to rain down on this town." He pivots on his heel and goes to walk out.

"Josh, wait!" I yell out. He turns his head and looks back at me, raising one eyebrow.

"You can't leave me here tied up like this, Joshua. Anyone could walk in and see me."

"Fuck!" He stomps over to me, his jaw clenched tight. He's angry. But I'm not afraid. Of all the people in the world I could choose not to be afraid of, it has to be him.

Once my arms are free, he rubs along my wrists, inspecting the red marks. "Wait here," he says as he runs out the gate. I pick up the discarded sweats and put them back on. I have to roll the waist over a few times so they don't fall down.

Grabbing the two sides of the ripped shirt, I tie them together in the middle, creating a little midriff top. Huh, it's actually not a bad look.

Josh comes back in, holding a riding jacket. He looks me up and down before saying, "Put this on."

It's pink, and clearly a female jacket. "No." I fold my arms over my chest. I am not putting on one of his floozies' jackets.

"What do you mean *no*? Put the fucking jacket on, Emmy. You are not walking out of this stable dressed like that. I can see... *everything*," he says.

"Really, well then, maybe you shouldn't have ripped my shirt. I am not wearing that. Deal with it." I stomp past him.

I don't get far before his arms come out, wrapping around my waist. He presses my back to his chest, bending his head to talk quietly into my ear.

"Emmy, there is a lot of staff on this property. Some I would hate to lose. But, so help me God, if anyone gets a glimpse of you like this, I will fucking cut their eyeballs out of their head before slitting their damn throats. You'd be surprised how hungry those pigs can get."

He lets go and smirks. Stepping in front of me, he holds out the jacket again.

"Your call, babe. What's it gonna be?" His eyebrows raise as he waits for an answer.

"You're not serious. You're not going to kill your staff just because they get a glimpse of my stomach." Even as I say the words, I know that his promises are not empty ones.

"Want to test the theory? I don't mind. Because at the end of the day, I'll still sleep at night—*with you right the fuck next to me.*"

Fuck it, I'm not going to have anyone else's blood on my conscience, especially someone who's innocent. Taking the jacket, I put it on and zip it up.

"You're fucking crazy, you know that." I stomp past him for the second time in a matter of minutes.

"Yeah, I've been told once or twice. But who's the crazier one here? Me, for being clinically insane, or you, for loving me that way?"

My steps momentarily stop. It's on the tip of my tongue, to refute his claims. To correct him. *Loved.* I loved him once, but I don't anymore. At least, that's what I've tried to convince myself. I don't say anything. Instead, I huff and storm towards the house with Josh hot on my trail.

CHAPTER EIGHT

JOSH

I followed Emily all the way through the house and into my bedroom. I don't even think she realises she automatically heads to my room, which I should really start thinking of as *our room*, considering I'm not ever letting her leave it.

I follow her across the room to the en suite door. She turns as she steps into the bathroom, sending me an icy as hell glare as she rips the jacket off and throws it at me, before she slams the door right in my face. I laugh, making sure she can hear it through the closed door.

The fact that she is beginning to stand up to me, beginning to feel comfortable around me, enough to be herself and not the scared girl I picked up from the woods two days ago... That fact is everything. I honestly didn't know how long she would be cowering from me. How long she would be afraid of what she says, afraid of what my reaction would be to the things she says or does.

Whatever she's been living through, I'm going to make sure it doesn't keep a hold on her. I wanted to climb inside her head last night, just to kill the demons that haunt her dreams for her. I hate that I can't fix that. I hate that she's dreaming about another man, even if it is a nightmare. No motherfucking other man should be taking up space inside her mind.

Fuck, I need to get my hands on this fucker. Pulling out my phone, I dial Sam. He picks up on the second ring.

"Why the fuck haven't you called me yet?" I yell through the phone.

"Well, hello to you too, boss. Good to see you're having a great day." He laughs.

"Fuck off, Sam. Start talking. What have you found?"

"Not much, which is why I haven't called. It seems Emily Livingston passed away at age twenty-two. Three years ago," he says.

"Well, obviously that's not fucking true. She's currently in my fucking bathroom."

"About that, I think I'll make a trip up there. Check this Emily out for myself, make sure you're not just, I don't know, batshit crazy and talking to the dead."

"Don't bother. I'm heading to the city tonight. I'll be

bringing her with me. What else did you find out? How did she supposedly die?"

"The coroner's report says suicide. Last known address was in Adelaide."

"Adelaide? What the fuck was she doing there?" Heading over to the little bar I keep in my bedroom, I pour a glass of whisky—it's five o'clock somewhere.

"There's something else," Sam says.

"Well, go on, mate. Don't hold back," I urge.

"There was a trust that one—Joshua McKinley—had set up in her name. She was due to get it when she turned twenty-two."

"Don't be a dick. I know about the fucking trust."

"Well, did you know it was emptied three years ago? One day before she apparently committed suicide?"

"I never bothered to check it," I admit.

"It was five million dollars, Josh. You never checked a bank account with five million dollars in it? Gee, guess that's how the other half rolls, hey?"

"Who made the withdrawal?" I ask.

"The name on the check is hers. Think she somehow managed to fake her own death? Maybe she ran out of money and that's why she's back?"

"No, she wouldn't do that. Send me a copy of the coroner's report." I hang up on him.

Within seconds, my phone buzzes in my hand with his email. Opening up the report, I have to remind myself it's fake. She's real. She's in my bathroom. Even I'm not so fucking crazy that I've conjured her up.

Emily comes out of the bathroom with a towel

wrapped around her, steam billowing all around her. Her blonde hair hangs down her back. She's every man's fucking wet dream. Those long, toned legs and slim waist...

She walks over to the bed and sits on the edge. Going into my wardrobe, I walk back out with a shirt for her to put on.

"We need to go shopping and get you some clothes of your own. As much as I love seeing you in my things, they're not going to work for every occasion." Handing her the shirt, I watch as she stares at me.

"Thank you, but you don't need to take me shopping. I'm fine." Her head lowers again as she wrings the fabric of the shirt between her fingers.

"Emmy?" I ask.

"Yeah?"

"Do you know anything about this?" Offering over my phone, I wait as she reads the report on the screen, her hands shaking.

"No, he wouldn't have... How could he? No." She shakes her head, tears forming in her eyes.

Kneeling down in front of her, I grab hold of her hands. They tremble under my touch.

"Emmy, it's okay. I can fix this. Whatever this is. I can fix it for you. You just have to tell me what you know."

"I... I don't know. I didn't know about this. I don't understand. I'm right here. Obviously, I'm not dead."

"Thank fuck for that." I swipe the lone tear that escapes down her cheek with my thumb. "Do you need money? Is that why you came here?" I prompt, feeling like a complete jerk for even asking her that.

"What? No. I don't need your money. I told you I can leave. I'll never bother you again. I don't need you to give me anything." She starts to stand up.

"I know. I just... You won't tell me a damn thing, Emmy, and I find out you were pronounced dead just a day after withdrawing five million dollars from your trust account? I don't know what to think here, Em."

"I don't know what this is," she says, waving my phone around. "But I didn't have a trust account. I was the scholarship kid, remember? Not a trust fund brat," she spits out at me.

"I set up a trust for you. You were able to access it the day you turned twenty-two. It appears you withdrew the whole amount in one go, then transferred it to an offshore account."

Emmy shakes her head. "No, I didn't. And why the hell would you set up a trust for me? Five million dollars? Really, Josh? What the hell would one person need that much money for?"

"I wanted to make sure you were taken care of. That you wouldn't ever need to worry about money again," I tell her.

She laughs, full-belly laughs. "That's funny. Because for the past three years, I haven't." Her mouth snaps shut.

"You haven't what?" I pry.

"Been alive apparently," she answers before

mumbling under her breath, "Ironically... it's not far from the truth."

This conversation is not going to get either of us anywhere. She doesn't know about the trust or the death certificate—*that* I'm sure of.

"Get dressed, you can find some sweats in the closet. We're going to the city," I say as I walk out the door.

━━━◯━━━

I'VE BEEN WAITING at the bottom of the stairs for thirty minutes. What the fuck could be taking her so long? I've had time to sort through some files, and pack my laptop and other essentials into a bag. All she had to do was throw on some sweatpants.

I'm about ready to go up and drag her out, when I hear her footsteps. Turning around, I see her coming down the steps. No. Fuck no!

She's put on a blue flannel shirt, and somehow tied a black belt around the middle of it. It looks like a dress. A short fucking dress that is showing off her every fucking curve. She's put her Converse back on her feet. Her hair, now dry, hangs in loose curls over one of her shoulders.

"That doesn't look like sweats," I grunt out.

Emily looks down at herself, running her hands over her body and smoothing out the flannel material.

"Mhm, I suppose it doesn't, considering, you know, it's not sweats." She shrugs.

It's a three-hour trip into the city. Deciding I don't really have time to win the argument about her putting more clothes on, I let it go. Or, more accurately, on the outside, I let it go. On the inside, I'm fucking seething at the thought of other people seeing that much of her skin.

"Emmy, whatever you do, don't let go of my hand," I tell her as I take hold of her open palm.

She looks up at me, confused, her eyebrows drawn down. "Why?"

"Because when you're touching me, I feel less murdery. Also, it's a little harder to slice someone's throat with just one hand, though not impossible. It just takes longer," I answer as I lead her outside to the waiting Range Rover.

She doesn't question me. What she does do is squeeze my hand tighter.

EMILY FELL ASLEEP an hour into the trip. Sitting in the back seat with her head resting on my shoulder, she never lets go of my hand. Even as she sleeps, she still has a tight grip on that hand.

She's been sleeping for the last hour and a half. Whatever's happening inside her head now is not peaceful. She's stirring, her body jerking around slightly. Her fingernails pierce into my skin to the point I can feel tiny drops of blood escape.

I should wake her up. That would be the right thing

to do. The only reason I'm not waking her from this nightmare is she's mumbling out incoherent words. I'm waiting for something to slip out of her mouth that I can actually use. Something to tell me what the fuck she's running from.

I sit still as her nails dig in, her head shaking no. She looks tortured; she looks like she's in hell right now. Sweat coats her forehead while blonde hair sticks to her face. If I was a better man, I'd wake her up. I'd stop this torture.

I've never pretended to be good. I'm not ashamed of who I am. A soul-tearing scream leaves her mouth before she bolts upright. "No, Trent, stop!" she screams.

Her eyes are staring ahead, but she's not fully awake. Finally, I have a fucking name. Not much to go on, but it's more than I had before.

"Emmy, it's okay. It's just a dream. You're safe," I whisper, as I pull her into my arms and give her the comfort I've been holding back. "You're safe; no one is going to hurt you ever again." Moving the hair off her face, I gently kiss her forehead as I whisper promises I'll die in order to keep.

"Josh?" she asks.

"Yeah, it's me. You're okay."

"I'm sorry. Did I wake you?" Why the fuck is she apologising to me?

"Emmy, you have nothing to be sorry about, babe. You didn't wake me, and even if you did, I wouldn't care."

My phone vibrates in my pocket. I shuffle as I

retrieve it. Emmy tries to move over. I have to grip her tighter as I bring the phone to my ear.

"Yeah."

"Boss, what did you want done with the occupant in the shed?" Paul asks.

"Fuck, I fucking forgot about that cocksucker." How the hell did I forget about the fucker that had Emmy held up in a stable this morning?

"Yeah, I figured you've got other things on your mind," Paul says.

"Keep him on ice. I'll only be gone a couple of days. I'll deal with him when I get back."

"Sure thing. Also, your mother just asked me about increasing security for the wedding. Congratulations," he says loudly through the phone. I know Emmy hears him when she tenses and looks away.

"It's not for me, asshole. It's for Dean's wedding."

I hang up. I don't need to be discussing details for a fucking wedding—not until it's my wedding we're planning.

"It seems my mother's planning a wedding for Dean and Ella. It's probably a good thing we got out of there. She would have ended up planning a double wedding. She's taken by the idea of you being her daughter-in-law." I smile at her. She does not smile back. Instead, she chooses to ignore me, changing the subject.

"Are we nearly there? Will we be seeing Dean and Ella when we're there?" she asks as she looks out the window.

"About fifteen minutes away. Do you want to see them?"

Emmy shrugs her shoulders. "I like Ella; she's nice."

"She is nice. Why the fuck she married Dean's ugly ass, I have no idea."

Emmy quickly turns her head in my direction as her eyes squint at me. "You and Ella seem close," she says.

"As close as two people can be who only just met weeks ago. I suppose."

"You don't like people, Josh. You've never been close to anyone. Well, at least you didn't used to. It's been a while so maybe you like people now. I don't know." Her rambling stops.

"Nope, still can't stand fucking people. They're a bunch of idiots. The only person I've ever liked is you, Emmy. You know that."

"And now Ella," she clarifies.

"And now Ella," I confirm, pausing a little. "Are you jealous that I'm friends with Ella?" I ask with the biggest smile on my face.

"What? No, I'm not bloody jealous. Curious is what I am, considering you never had any friends in school. Not that you ever wanted friends… though I can guarantee any one of the girls back then would have chopped off a limb to be *friends* with you." She frames the word "friends" with air quotes.

"Ella's my sister, Emily. There is absolutely no reason for you to be jealous of anyone. No one has ever been able to measure up to you."

"I'm not jealous. I can see why you'd be friends with Ella. I mean, it's been a long time since I've had any friends, but I can see she would be a good one to have."

"Why haven't you had any friends, Emmy. You were always surrounded by people at school. It seemed everyone wanted to be your best friend back then."

"They weren't really my friends, Josh. They were just too scared of what you would do to them if they weren't. People had this assumption that if they were friends with me, you'd leave them be. God only knows why they thought that—it's not like *I* was spared from your torture."

"Trust me, babe, I spared you in high school."

"You literally tipped a milkshake over my head the first time we met." She holds up one finger before she continues. "Then there was that time you got me kicked off the cheerleading team. I still don't know how you managed that, but I know it was you." Her second finger goes up.

I smile at the fond memory. "I bribed the coach. But, in my defence, that uniform showed off way too much skin," I argue.

"You weren't my boyfriend, Josh. You wouldn't even speak to me."

"I was trying to save you from me."

The third finger goes up. "The time you put red hair dye in my shampoo. My hair was bloody bright red. Do you have any idea how embarrassed I was to walk out of the girls' locker room that day? That shit stayed in my hair for months."

"I thought it would make you uglier, less appealing to others. That one backfired because you looked hot as fuck with that fiery red hair. Do you know how many guys I beat up in those few months? My knuckles were constantly fucking bruised."

Emmy's mouth hangs open as she shakes her head. "That, just—wow. You're just... Wow," she says, then holds up a fourth finger. "The time you slashed my tyres."

"That was your fault."

"How do you figure that?" she asks.

"You offered Jackson a ride home that day."

"So, I do a good deed for someone and you decide that I needed to be punished for that?" Her eyebrows go up to her hairline.

"Not punished. Just stopped from having another guy in your car. Besides, I made sure you had a ride home that day *and* I replaced your tyres."

"You had your limo driver take me home. Do you have any idea how embarrassing that was? To turn up in my neighbourhood in a damn limo?"

"Emily, you lived in the suburbs, not the fucking Bronx."

"Doesn't matter. It was embarrassing." She holds up a fifth finger. I take hold of her hand, stopping her.

"As much as I'd love to continue this trip down memory lane, because really there are so many fond memories of us during those high school years, we're here. Come on."

"You do realise those fond memories are all one-sided in your own head, right? Those moments weren't *fond* for me at all," she says as she climbs out of the car. I have to step in front of her to prevent someone from getting a view of her ass.

If I thought I'd get any peace tonight, I was mistaken. As soon as we step through the lobby, we're greeted by Sam and Tony. Tony is Sam's assistant. I've never liked the prick, but I like him even less right now with the way he's looking at Emmy.

CHAPTER NINE

EMILY

*J*osh pulls me slightly behind him as we enter the lobby, or yet another museum-lookalike building. He stops in front of two hulking men in suits. My first thought is maybe they've found me—they're probably detectives. Then Josh shakes the hand of one.

"Sam, what the fuck are you doing here?" he asks.

The guy Sam looks directly at me behind Josh and smiles. "First, I wanted to make sure you weren't conjuring up the dead. Now that that's settled, I have some documents that need your signature." He waves a briefcase in the air.

The other guy stares at me, and not in a friendly way. It creeps me out. I step further behind Josh, trying to escape the man's gaze.

"It couldn't have waited until tomorrow?" Josh asks as he starts heading towards the elevator, pulling me along with him. The two men follow close behind.

"No, it couldn't. It's the Casey merger. It needs to be finalised today," Sam says as we all enter the lift.

Josh steps behind me, wraps an arm around my waist and pulls my back against his chest. As the doors shut, he buries his head in the crook of my neck. I hear him inhale before he whispers in my ear, "Emmy, I really need you to hold my hand right now."

My eyes go wide. I look up, staring at our reflection on the metal doors. I place both of my hands in his. One hand curls over the fingers holding my hip, while the other grabs the hand hanging down at his side. I squeeze tight.

I can feel his hands trembling. What the fuck happened out there that's got him this messed up? It can't be the fact that he has to sign papers. Surely that's the kind of thing he does all the time.

I watch the numbers as the elevator travels up. I know we're heading to the penthouse by the PH button that Sam pressed. My thumbs rub tiny circles on Josh's hand. I'm not sure what to do to help him. I do know that I *want* to help him. I shouldn't want to, but I do.

I really need to find a way to get away from him. The longer I'm around, the further I slip into the Josh fog. That place where I can pretend that everything is normal, that we have a chance at a future together. I'm constantly reminding myself that we don't, that I can't have that.

It's better for everyone if I disappear... *sooner rather than later*. Even as I tell myself this, my heart is hurting. Josh was right. There was a reason that I came to him. That when I finally got free, the first place I thought to go was that damn cabin. The first person that I wanted to see was Josh. Not that I can ever admit any of this to him.

The elevator finally stops, and the doors open. I release the breath I didn't even know I was holding. Stepping out of the lift, I don't let go of Josh's hand. He leads me further into the room. It's elegance at its finest. It's McKinley-level elegance. The foyer where we are standing is white, white, and more white. White marble floors, pristine white walls. We're standing under a huge sparkling crystal chandelier; the thing looks bigger than me.

Past the foyer, the floor steps down into a living room. White leather couches face each other with a grey marble coffee table between them. Beyond the couches are floor-to-ceiling windows—the view currently being obstructed by sheer (yep, you guessed it) white curtains.

All the white and light is such a contrast to how I would have imagined Josh's place. I feel so out of sorts here, like I'm going to mess something up or break something I can't afford.

Yeah, like I've been able to afford *anything* for the past three years. I met Trent four years ago—the first year was perfect. He had me completely fooled. The last three years were utter hell. I wasn't allowed out of the apartment, unless I was with him. I wasn't allowed to have access to money. I didn't even own a purse. The thought of not being able to afford something is laughable. I can't even afford a damn happy meal at this point.

The little amount of money I took from our apartment didn't go far. I think I have around five dollars left and tucked into the lining of my backpack, which has been shoved into the corner of Josh's closet.

"Emmy, the kitchen is just through there. Go get yourself a drink, or whatever you want." Josh lets go of me and points towards an entryway off to the left of the room.

I nod my head. I wouldn't mind a moment alone anyway—some time to get out of the Josh fog. As I'm about to walk in the direction that Josh pointed, Sam steps in front of me. I have to tilt my head up to meet his eyes.

"Since this asshole doesn't have any fucking manners, I'll introduce myself. I'm Sam, Josh's friend." He holds his hand out to me in greeting, a hand which I have no intention of shaking.

Instead, I put my hands in my pockets. Who the fuck does he think he is, calling Josh an asshole and talking about his lack of social skills? It makes me want to knee him in the nuts.

"I'm Emily. But you already know that, I'm sure. I would advise you though, if you ever want the chance to father children in the future, I'd refrain from calling Josh an asshole or making comments on his social skills. If he wanted me to meet you, he would have introduced us."

I'm not sure where my sudden courage to speak to anyone like this has come from. Maybe Josh is rubbing off on me more than I thought. Deep down, I do know I'm safe if Josh is around. Maybe that's why I feel like I can say what's on my mind.

As I go to walk around the jerk, I'm pulled back by Josh, who spins me around so fast I lose my footing. His arm goes around my waist, steadying me while also pulling me tight against his chest.

My first thought is that I've made a mistake. I've made him mad. I should have kept my mouth shut and been polite to his friend. All those thoughts get blown out of my head when his lips descend onto mine, his tongue hungrily diving into my mouth.

I don't know if it's relief I feel or just my pure wanton need for the man, which makes me pull him closer, desperately trying to climb into his skin as I return his kiss tenfold. A little groan leaves his mouth as he pulls away from me.

Josh smiles down at me. "Want me to turn him into pig feed?" he asks, as he nods his head to Sam.

I look over my shoulder at Sam and consider Josh's offer, or at least pretend to consider it. "Tough call, but you should probably keep him around. I'm going to see what I can find in the kitchen. I'm suddenly starved," I say, as I walk past Sam and the weird guy who's creeping me out by just standing in the background and staring. Even as I walk away, I can feel his beady eyes pinned to my back.

⬂

I'VE JUST OPENED the fridge when I hear Sam shout out, "Josh, stop. Don't do it!"

I shut the door and tiptoe back out to the living room, where I can see that Josh has the creepy guy by the throat and up against the pristine white wall. It's not the tattooed hand wrapped around his throat that has me frozen to my spot. It's the gun Josh is holding to the man's head.

"Give me one good reason why I shouldn't blow your fucking brains out right now?" Josh seethes.

"I-I'm sorry. I didn't mean any disrespect, sir," the guy stammers out.

"Disrespect? You've been nothing but disrespectful since the moment we stepped through the lobby downstairs. Do you think I haven't noticed the way you were looking at her? Do you take me for a fucking fool? Think I don't know the thoughts running through your head?" Josh screams in his face.

"No, I didn't. *I don't.*" He shakes his head.

Holy shit, this is about me. Josh is losing his shit over me. I should say something, put a stop to this. I knew something was eating at him in the elevator, but I didn't think it would be because someone was looking at me. Even though I know I should try to stop this, my feet are frozen in place, fear gripping me. What if he blames me? What if he thinks this is all my fault? I should have worn the sweats like he wanted me to.

"Josh, man, calm down. Put the gun away. You don't want to do this in front of your girl." Sam nods his head towards me.

Josh turns and looks at me. "Fuck!" he mumbles out, as he lets go of the guy before stepping back. He holds the gun down by the side of his leg, tapping it repeatedly against his thigh. I'm afraid he's going to accidentally shoot himself if he keeps doing that, yet I'm still frozen to my spot. I still can't seem to make my feet move. They should be running the hell out of here. Any reasonable, sane person would be running out of here.

"Fuck, man, you're batshit crazy over a damn bitch. Talk about being fucking pussy-whipped. Must be a fucking gold-plated pussy," the creepy guy, who has just been renamed in my head as *dumbass*, spits out.

Josh raises the gun up and shoots, hitting the man's left kneecap. He doesn't even blink as the guy falls to the ground. "That was a warning shot, motherfucker. The next one will be in your fucking head."

The guy is rolling around on the ground, screaming incoherent nonsense—the once pristinely white floor and wall now covered in blood. Josh turns and looks me up and down.

"Clean this mess, and shut him the fuck up, before I do it permanently," he says to Sam as he walks slowly towards me. This is the moment I should run; in my head, I know that. But my heart, it wants something completely different. It wants the devil who's making his way to me, slowly, carefully, like I'm a wounded animal about to take flight. I fear it's too late to run—even if I could, I'm not sure I would.

"Emmy." Josh takes a breath in, releasing it slowly before continuing, "I'm sorry. You shouldn't have had to see that." He's standing in front of me, apologising.

I nod my head. I don't know what to say. His grey sweats and white shirt are now stained with blood and he's still clenching the gun in his hand. Yet, all I can think is how badly I want to climb him, claim him as mine.

My thighs tighten together as I feel myself getting wetter and wetter by the minute. I'm not wearing any underwear, and I'm at risk of having my desire run down my inner thighs right now. I can feel my hardened nipples rubbing against the flannelette fabric of the shirt.

"Josh, where's the bedroom?" I ask.

He nods his head behind me. "Down that way. Why?" he says with a smirk.

"I-I'm going to need you to take me there now," I whisper.

Josh wraps one arm around me and picks me up. My legs encircle his waist and cling on. My hands go to his hair as my mouth finds his. His groans of pleasure run through me as he walks us down a hall.

I'm so lost in all that is Josh that when I'm thrown down on a bed, confusion and dizziness take over as I open my eyes. Josh is standing at the end of the bed, pulling his shirt over his head.

I lick my lips as his perfectly-sculpted, tanned body comes into view. I really need to book an appointment with him. Hours long, where I can run my tongue along all those grooves. Draw the outline of those tattoos that cover him with (yep, you guessed it) my tongue.

Even as I lie here, conjuring up all of the things I want to do to his body, I know it's wrong. I know that it's only going to hurt more when everything I've done comes crashing down on me, on him, and ends up ruining us.

"I fear the longer I keep you, the more I'm going to ruin you," Josh confesses as if reading my inner thoughts.

"And just how do you suppose you're going to ruin me exactly?" I ask.

"My darkness is going to overtake your light; my darkness is going to ruin every good thing there is inside you. I can see it's already happening. Yet, I can't seem to let you go. I won't ever let you go again, Emmy."

"You can't ruin me, Josh. I'm already ruined."

"No, you're not, but you will be." He smirks as he strips off his sweats.

He doesn't know that he already ruined me in this way... years ago. I've never wanted anyone the way I want Josh. Even in the beginning with Trent, when it was good, it wasn't Josh-level good.

Josh climbs on the bed and undoes the belt, his belt, from around my waist. "As much as I want to tie you up and have you at my mercy, I want to feel your hands all over me. I want to feel those nails scratching my back when I make you come like you've never come before," he says as he throws the belt across the room.

He climbs up and straddles my thighs, slowly reaching for the top of the shirt. He undoes one button at a time. What happened to just ripping the damn thing open? I'm all for that right now. But no, he ever so slowly undoes one, then the next. When he gets to the last button and spreads the shirt apart, his eyes go wide.

"Fuck, Emmy, you've been naked ever since we left the house. How the fuck have you been naked this whole time and I didn't know?"

I'm not sure if he's asking me, or himself. I answer anyway. "I wasn't naked. I had a shirt on."

"You're not wearing panties, Emily. That's naked!" Josh emphasises the word *naked*. "If I had known I had unrestricted access to this sweet-ass pussy of yours the whole way here, it would have been a much more pleasurable car ride." His fingertips twist and pull on my nipples as he talks.

My back arches off the bed. "Oh yeah, with your driver watching through the rear-view mirror?" I ask.

"Sure, why not?"

"You'd seriously let someone watch you strip me naked and fuck me in the car?" I don't know why the idea is so damn appealing, but I'm locking that shit down tight, shoving the idea in the vault for another time.

"Yep, I'd cut their fucking eyes out afterwards, but I'd let them watch." He shrugs as he brings his mouth down onto my nipple.

They're so sensitive. I'm a squirming, begging mess within minutes of his mouth taking turns at torturing each nipple. As much as I try to move, I can't. He's still straddling me. My hands pull at his hair, alternating between trying to pry his mouth away from me and pulling him even closer.

I'm out of my mind with need. "Josh, please, I need…"

He lets go of my nipple, a plop sound echoing in the room. "What do you need, Emmy?" he asks.

He's going to make me say it. Asshole. He knows what I need. He always knows what I need.

"I need you. I need you inside me now, damn it," I scream.

"Babe, all you had to do is ask. I'm not a mind read-er." The bastard smirks. Moments later, he jumps off and flips me over, positioning me on my knees with my ass up in the air.

Josh's hands spread my cheeks open. I feel his tongue lick from top to bottom, right along my slit. My fingers curl around the sheets. I'm trembling. I'm ready to burst. When I feel the tip of his cock at my entrance, I push back.

I can't wait any longer. As soon as his cock bottoms out inside me, the moment it rubs along my G-spot, I lose all control. I scream as my pussy convulses around him.

"Fuck, Em, I fucking love how hungry your pussy is for my cock. Hold on, babe, the show is only just beginning," he says, right before he starts to slam in and out of my still quivering core.

CHAPTER TEN

JOSH

I watch Emily sleep peacefully next to me. She passed out shortly after her sixth orgasm. She's so fucking beautiful it hurts. I can't believe I let her go all those years ago. I've wasted so much time. She's obviously endured a lot of crap that she shouldn't have. And she wouldn't have, had I manned up and kept her like I wanted to.

Tugging the sheets higher, I cover her up as I stand, gently kissing her forehead before I slip out of the room. As much as I want to stay curled up in this little world with her, and just her, I've got shit to sort out. Sam mentioned the Casey merger, which is code for *confidential*, and not necessarily something that's work-related.

Fuck, I hope he's got a better lead on who the fuck

has been abusing Emily for God knows how long. I make my way out to the kitchen; I need a fucking drink. Of course, I find Sam, cooking some shit that smells fucking delicious on the stove.

"Make yourself at home, mate," I say as I walk past him to the fridge. Grabbing the OJ, I drink from the bottle, not bothering with a glass.

"Don't worry, I will," Sam replies.

"What'd you do with Tony?" Not that I really care, but I'd like to know the fucker is not still in the apartment. Not still in the same space as me. Even with Emily draining me of every bit of fucking energy, I'm still buzzing to cause damage to that fucker—well, more damage than I did by blowing out his kneecap.

"Clean up crew. He'll be fine," Sam says. "I, however, am now in need of yet another new assistant. Thanks for that," he grunts.

"*Please*, I did you a favour. What else have you got for me?"

"Not much—found a death certificate for her mother, dated two years ago."

"Fuck, I was wondering why she didn't turn to her mum for help."

"That's not all. Mum didn't cark it; she's alive and breathing. Same address you gave me as Emily's last known."

"What the fuck does that mean? Who the fuck's out there writing up death certificates for people who are fucking alive and breathing?"

"No idea, man. That's all I got. Everything's been

buried bloody good. It seems someone didn't want anyone finding these documents. She tell you anything yet?" he asks.

"No, I've stopped asking. She did let a name slip in her sleep though," I say, remembering the nightmare she had in the car.

"Care to share?" Sam prompts, as he serves up three plates of what looks like some kind of stir fry concoction.

"Trent." I raise my eyebrows at him. "You expecting company?" I nod at the three plates.

"Nope, but you gotta eat. And I'm not gonna lie. I think I like Emily more than I like you. And it seems I have some serious grovelling to do to win her over."

"She's asleep. You're out of luck." I smirk, recalling just what exhausted her to sleepiness.

He hands me a plate and fork, walking around my fucking kitchen like he owns the place. "Eat," he says, as he picks up another plate and fork before heading out of the kitchen.

"Where are you going?" I ask him.

"To wake her up. She needs to eat," he offers simply.

"Take another step towards that bedroom and I'll fucking shoot you," I warn him. Like fuck, I'm about to let him walk in there while she's fucking naked. Just the thought of a naked Emily makes my cock hard.

"Fine, but when she wakes up, make sure she knows I cooked this shit for her, not you." He places cling wrap over the plate before putting it in the fridge.

"Why do you care if she likes you anyway?" I ask.

"Because she scares the shit out of me," he admits.

I laugh. How the hell can a tiny little Emily scare the shit out of a six-foot something hulk of a man? "How so?"

He looks me in the eye, quiet for a moment, then with all seriousness, he says, "She'd only have to say the word and you'd slice my fucking throat for her, without a second thought."

I'd like to say he's wrong. But he's not. So, instead, I just dig into the food. He's one hell of a cook. I'll give him that.

"So, Trent…? Did you happen to get a last name, or are we just going to run around the country burying every fucker named Trent?" Sam asks.

"No last name," I grunt. I'm fucking pissed that I don't know who the fuck I need to kill yet.

I hear the bell on the lift ping, and groan when I look at the screen on the wall showing me who just arrived. Fucking Whitney.

I listen for the sound of her heels clicking against the marble floors as she makes her way through the apartment to the kitchen.

She stops short when she sees me and Sam. "Josh, I heard you were back in town." She plasters on what is supposed to be a seductive smile. All it's doing is making my cock, which was hard minutes ago, fucking limp—and to think, I used to fuck this bitch.

"What the fuck are you doing here, Whitney?" I growl.

"I came to see you, silly. I thought we could have

some fun." She places her hand on my chest. Sam chokes on his mouthful of food as he tries not to laugh.

"Yeah, well, you thought wrong. Leave," I tell her, removing her hand from my chest.

"Come on, Josh, you know I'll make you feel good." Her hand runs up my thigh and begins to rub my cock. I'm wondering what I ever fucking saw attractive about her when Sam coughs loudly, gaining my attention. I look at him and he nods behind me.

I don't even have to look to know who's there. *Emily*. And she's watching another woman rub her hands all over me right now. Fuck. I push Whitney off me as I jump up and turn to Emily, except she's already walking back down towards the bedroom.

Following, I get to the room just as she's turning to walk back out, only now she's holding a gun in her hands. My gun. The sight of Emmy pointing a gun at me should not turn me the fuck on right now, but it fucking does.

I make no attempt to hide the fact that I have to readjust my cock, my boner standing tall and proud. The disgusted look that crosses over Emmy's face tells me she's less than impressed.

"Move out of my way, Josh," she says as she points the gun right at my chest. Her hands are frighteningly steady.

"You'll have to shoot me if you think I'm going to let you walk out of here." I fold my arms over my chest and stand in the doorway.

Emily tilts her head and stares at me. Fuck, I think she's actually contemplating fucking shooting me.

"Why? It's obvious you don't need me here. Not even an hour after you've used every inch of my body, you have one of your whores at your beck and call. The bed's not even fucking cold yet, Joshua!" she screams. I can't help but smile at her jealousy. Fucking finally, she's letting her feelings for me show.

"What the fuck are you smiling at?" she asks.

"You're jealous. But I've told you before. You don't need to be, Emmy. Nobody will ever measure up to you. I didn't invite her here. I told her to leave. You can ask Sam if you don't believe me," I offer.

"You asked her to leave, yet she was still standing there rubbing you up and down to the point that you're now in front of me with a fucking hard-on." She points the gun in the direction of my cock.

Okay, that's a little much. "Babe, if you're going to shoot me, then do it anywhere other than there. Please," I practically beg. "I told her to leave. *This.*" I point to my hard-on. "...is because of *you*. You standing here pointing a gun at me is hot as hell."

"You're demented," she huffs like it's not old news. "If you really did ask her to leave, then you won't mind if I go out there and shoot her, instead of you."

"Be my guest." I wave my arm and step out of the doorway. She smiles and walks past me. Well, fuck. That backfired. I didn't think she'd actually walk out there.

I follow close behind her. I'm a little intrigued at

119

how this will play out. I'm not about to let her shoot someone though. I know she'll regret it later. She has way too much of a conscience for that shit.

Emily stands in front of Whitney. "I don't think Josh wants you here. You need to leave." She speaks clearly, calmly.

Whitney laughs. "Oh, hunny, I think you're the one that needs to leave. Josh, did you let Sam bring in the trash again?"

"Maybe all the Botox has fried your brain cells, so I'll tell you again. *You need to leave.*" Emily points the gun at her.

Whitney gasps as she eyes the other end of the barrel. "Josh, are you seriously going to let this bitch threaten me?"

Okay, I've heard enough. I was ready to see how far Emily would take this. But Whitney has said one too many things about my girl for my liking.

I'm quick to step in front of Emily as my hand wraps around Whitney's ponytail. "You see, I was prepared to let you walk out of here unscathed. *Mostly.* But then you had to go and open your mouth and talk shit about my girl."

Whitney's eyes go wide. "You can't seriously want *that...* over me." She's so fucking dumb. She doesn't know when the fuck to shut up. As much as I want to snap her neck, I'm trying to not let my darkness rub off on Emily more than it already has. Bloodshed and dead bodies should not be normal, everyday occurrences in her life.

"Sam, escort the trash out. Make sure she can't get back in." I watch as Whitney smiles, until Sam comes up and grabs her by the arm and starts leading her out.

Turning around, I see Emily now sitting on the couch, the gun in front of her on the coffee table. I go and sit down next to her, pulling her into my arms. She comes willingly, thank God.

Holding her head to my chest, I wait for her to say something. After a few minutes, she speaks, but doesn't move. "Josh, I'm scared," she says so quietly.

"What are you scared of, Emmy?" I ask, wanting to slay all of her fucking demons.

"I'm scared I'm not going to be able to let you go again when the time comes."

"That time's never going to come, Emmy. I'm not letting you go." I kiss the top of her head.

"You'll think differently soon. I'm not the same person I was in high school."

"I'll never think any differently of you than how I already do, than what I always have. You are perfection, Emily."

"I hope you're right," she whispers.

"I know I am. I am very rarely wrong, you know." I smile.

"In your head, maybe. But you were very wrong that time you thought I was dating Jimmy. You scared the poor kid out of school."

"I did, didn't I? And if you weren't dating him, then why the fuck did he think he could put his arm around you constantly?"

"He did that one time, Josh. And I was certainly not dating him. He was way more into you than me." She laughs.

"What?"

"He was gay. As in, had a bigger crush on you than I did back then."

"Wait, you had a crush on me? How did I not know that?" I ask sarcastically.

Sam walks back into the apartment and heads straight to the kitchen. As he passes us, he yells out to me, "If you don't bring her in here to eat, I'm going to bring the food to her."

Emily's head pops up; her eyebrows draw down. "Does he have a weird food fetish I should be aware of?"

I laugh. "No, he's just trying to win you over. He's afraid if he doesn't, I'm gonna end up shooting him or something."

"Oh, okay. Well, I'll be nicer to him, put his mind at ease," she says as she jumps off my lap.

"Where are you going?"

"To eat. I'm starving." She heads into the kitchen.

I enter right behind her. Sam places a plate of food down on the bench next to my half-eaten meal.

"Do you want a drink, Emily?" he asks her.

"Ah, sure, water's fine." Emily says, looking between the two of us. She smirks at me before walking up to Sam, who hands her a bottle of water.

She wraps her arms around him. "Thank you so much, Sam. I can't believe how good this food smells."

Sam eyes me. Holding his hands out to the side, he doesn't return the hug. But that doesn't deter Emily from attempting to push my buttons, even though I know what she's doing.

"I don't think anyone's ever cooked for me before," she says.

"I made you cookies that one time in year eleven," I remind her.

She spins around, folding her arms over her chest. "That was you? *Of course,* it was you. Who else would give me Valentine's Day cookies that were full of laxatives!"

"I saved you from a disastrous date with Matthew. I heard he was trying to take you out to the old rock. You know, people only went there for one reason, Emmy," I tell her.

She shakes her head no. "What if I wanted to go to the old rock with Matty? What if I wanted him to do unspeakable things to me in the back of his BMW? He was on the football team after all."

I raise an eyebrow at her. "Did you? Did you want Matthew to do unspeakable things to you, Emmy?" I ask, ready to hunt the fucker down and do *unspeakable things* to him.

"Ah, no?" she questions.

"Right answer."

"You know you two are fucking twisted as shit, right?" Sam says as he sits on the bench and continues eating.

"Wait, *him*, I get. But what's wrong with me?" Emmy

123

asks as she sits down. I sit next to her and drag her chair over so she's much closer to me.

Sam laughs at her question. "That's a loaded gun, babe. I'm not answering that."

My fork flies across the room, barely missing his head. "I won't miss next time, fucker. Her name is fucking Emily!" I grunt.

Emily grabs hold of my hand. "Joshua, stop tormenting the one person who is probably your only friend. I like him. I think we'll keep him around." She smiles at me.

"Yep, well, on that note, I'm out of here while I'm still fucking alive. Josh, I'll see you in the office tomorrow." *Yeah, I know.* I'll be there.

CHAPTER ELEVEN

EMILY

I'm woken up by something tickling my face. Scratch that, something sloppily kissing my face. I swipe at the culprit, groaning as I roll over and try to escape. Then I realise my mistake and jump up. "I'm sorry. I'm sorry. I'm awake," I say, as I wipe at my eyes.

My vision starts to focus in on the room. I'm not at home. It's okay. I look up into a pair of blue eyes. Blue eyes that are staring at me with concern, while a storm is brewing within them in the background.

Did I make him mad? I don't know what to do. I don't know what I'm supposed to do, so I pull the sheet up to my chest and sit there. I should make breakfast. I can make myself useful if I make breakfast.

"Emmy, stop. Whatever thoughts are going through

your pretty little head right now, tell 'em they can fuck right off. You're here with me. You're okay."

"Do you want breakfast? I can cook," I offer, not willing to share what exactly those thoughts were.

"We'll get something on the road. I gotta go into the office for a few hours. Come on, I want you to come with me," he says.

Now that I'm fully awake, I notice that he's in a suit, a really nice freaking suit. A charcoal jacket and pants with a white business shirt and light grey tie. He's wearing a tie. Josh, my Josh, does not wear ties. What happened to the ripped jeans and sweats?

"Why do you look like that?" I ask.

Josh glances down at himself. "I have to go into the office. I'm the boss, Em. I have to wear a suit."

"Yeah, but do you have to wear it that well? I mean, surely we can find you like an oversized jacket or something. I hear plaid is back in style," I offer up suggestions.

Josh smirks at me and stands up, doing a complete three-sixty. I get the full, head to toe view. Okay, my eyes didn't make it to the toes; they got stuck on the ass. Damn, what an ass that is.

"My eyes are up here, Emmy." Josh laughs as he catches me staring.

"Uh?" I pretend to play dumb. I *am* blonde, so it should work.

He shakes his head. "Come on, get up. As much as I love you naked, you need clothes on. You're coming with me," he says.

"Wait, what? I can't go to work with you. I'll just be in the way." Think, Emily, you have to get out of this. You cannot go into an office building and risk being seen.

"You're never in the way. I want you there," he argues.

"Josh, I'm tired. I'd rather stay here and wait for you to come back." I pray he will let me just stay locked up in this tower. It's much safer than being out and about in the city, in broad daylight.

"Besides, I have no clothes suitable to wear to an office." That's not a lie. I literally have no clothes on me. I don't know what he did with the jeans and sweatshirt I left in his bathroom that first day he found me.

Josh contemplates his options for a minute before pulling his phone out and calling someone.

"Ella, how's my favourite sister-in-law?" he asks.

I can't hear what she says back to him, as I'm only getting the one-sided conversation.

"Still counts. I need you to come over to my apartment and show Emily around some shops. She hasn't been out in the city and I don't want her getting lost."

My eyes go wide, and I shake my head. I am not going shopping. No way, no how.

"Now would be good. Tell him he'll manage." Josh hangs up the phone.

"I'm only going to be gone for a few hours. Ella's going to take you shopping. I'll wait for her to get here before I leave." He comes and sits on the bed. I start to shake my head no and protest.

"You need clothes, Emmy," he says as he pulls out a shiny black card from his wallet. "Take this—there's no limit on it." He grabs my hand and wraps it around the card.

"I-I'm not sure I can go shopping, Josh. I haven't been out to the shops for a really long time. What if I can't do it? What if something happens? I'd rather just stay here." My breathing picks up at the thought of being out in public, of being caught.

"Okay, how about I set the computer up, and you and Ella can do some online shopping? Have it delivered to the farm. We'll be back there tomorrow."

I nod my head. I have no intention of spending his money, but if it means I can escape the conversation, I'll agree to it.

"Do, um, do you want me to cook you breakfast before you go?" I ask.

"Emmy, you don't have to do anything you don't want to do. I'm a grown-ass man, capable of getting my own food if I have to. If you want to cook, then by all means, go and cook. If not, then don't. I don't want you to do anything you don't want to be doing," he says as he brushes the hair away from my forehead.

"Okay," I whisper. I'm just more confused now. I don't know what the right thing to do is. Yesterday, I felt so confident. I felt almost like myself again. Then, today, I wake up as the girl who's afraid to make her shadow appear on the wall the wrong way. I can't keep up.

"Emmy?" Josh asks.

"Yeah?"

"Promise me you'll be here when I get back." His voice is husky and vulnerable.

"I promise that if I'm not here, it's not because I didn't want to stay. The only thing that could get me out of this apartment today is if I'm dragged out." I give him the best I can offer.

"No one's going to be dragging you out of here, Emmy. You can't get up here without passing security and having the passcode, which I've just changed by the way. You are safe here." As he talks, he pulls out his phone, firing off a few text messages.

I don't bother to correct him. I know it's only a matter of time before everything catches up with me. I just hope that I don't end up destroying him in the process. I'm selfish to want to stay as long as I can. I know the longer I stick around, the harder it's going to be when we get torn apart.

Josh puts his phone away and walks into his closet, coming back out with a shirt and sweats.

"You should definitely change into that," I say, pointing at the clothes he's holding. "It's much more suitable attire."

He smirks at me. "These are for you. I'm sure you don't want to be naked when Ella arrives. Come on, I'll make you coffee."

I just stare at him. When was the last time someone made me coffee? I can't even recall. I had coffee yesterday with Josh's mum, but her chef made it. No wonder Josh doesn't want me to cook for him. He's grown up with five-star chefs cooking his every bloody meal. I'm such an idiot, thinking he'd want to eat anything I made.

"Sure," I say as I climb out of bed and take the clothes into the bathroom.

Closing the door behind me, I lean against it and stare at my reflection in the mirror. It's not until I'm alone, in this quiet space, that I let the tears fall. I've always been good at hiding my emotions and faking happiness. I've done it my whole life. But when I'm alone, I don't need to pretend to be happy, to be normal.

As I look in the mirror, I don't recognise the woman staring back at me. The bruising on my face has dimmed to a pale yellow. It won't be much longer until it's gone, although the scars will always be there, both physically and mentally.

I'm surprised Josh hasn't asked about them yet. I know he sees the scars from the numerous stitches I've had. He's licked and kissed over them, but hasn't asked.

Wiping the tears from my face, I freshen myself up and get dressed in Josh's clothes. I can smell him on the shirt. I bring it close to my nose and inhale, his scent having a somewhat calming effect on me. I brush my hair with the hairbrush that's been left on the counter. It's new, still in a packet. Did Josh leave this for me? Does he think I need to be better presented? That's probably why he wants me to go shopping with his money. He is a McKinley; they do have an image to uphold.

What kind of image does it give him to be seen with me? An unkempt, domestic violence victim—no, not a victim, *a survivor*. I am a survivor. Even if I did have to kill Trent to escape him, I managed to get myself free. I survived years of torture from that asshole. I need to get out of my own head and stop second guessing myself.

Opening the door, I find the bedroom empty. I make the bed and pick up yesterday's discarded clothes, placing them in the laundry hamper before I go off in search of Josh. I find him in the kitchen, cooking eggs. He looks... I'm not sure what the word is... But seeing him dressed in that damn suit and standing over the stove cooking eggs, I'm suddenly hungry for something that's not food.

He hears me enter and turns around. He gives me a once-over, from head to toe, and his jaw clenches. I can't bring myself to meet his eyes. I don't know what I've done wrong. I can never tell with Josh, and it makes me nervous as hell. Did I take too long in the bathroom?

He puts down the spatula and walks over to me. It takes everything in me not to back away. This is Josh. He's not Trent. He is not going to hurt me. In my heart, I know that he won't hurt me, but in my head, there's always that little fight or flight button telling me to fly.

Josh brings his hand up to my face, and although he does it slowly, I still flinch away from him. I close my eyes and, like all those times before, wait for the slap... but it never comes. His fingers brush underneath my eyes. Blinking them open, I see a whole whirlwind of emotions staring back at me. He's fighting with his own feelings just as much as I'm fighting with mine.

"You've been crying. I don't like it," he says as he pecks the softest of kisses under my eyes, while his tender touch only makes them water more. I don't understand his feelings towards me, when he clearly can't stand anyone else.

"Why do you like me, Josh?" I blurt out.

He's taken aback by the question and stares at me for a moment before answering. "Why do I like you? That's like asking why is the sky blue, babe. It just is. I don't know how to answer that. But I do know from the first day you made the terrible mistake of sitting at my table, you sealed your fate. Something inside me clicked for the first time in my life. I didn't know or understand what was happening at the time. I even talked to my mum about it. She was drunk, so it's probably a conversation she doesn't remember happening. But she cried and told me that I loved you—that's why I felt this overwhelming urge to protect you and make sure nothing bad ever happened to you."

He takes a breath in before continuing, "I don't just like you, Emmy. I love you. I always have. We both know that. Nobody gets me like you do. When you're around, I feel almost normal. I don't feel like I have to pretend to fit in with you because we just fit together."

I think about all that he said. "She remembers, you know? Your mum... I did know you loved me. I also knew you didn't want to. So, why now?"

He shrugs. "I've been going through life for the past seven years in black and white. The moment I heard your voice over the phone, my world became colourful again. I'm not giving you up for a second time, Emmy."

"Sometimes we don't get to choose our fates, Josh."

He doesn't get a chance to answer as smoke starts filling the room. Josh rushes over and turns off the stove, placing the frying pan in the sink. I wait for the yelling to start, the blaming me. Even though I wasn't the one cooking, I had distracted him.

I have to fix it. I have to make it right. "I'll fix it. Go sit down. I'll make something new," I say as calmly as I can while I open the fridge, inspecting what ingredients I have to work with.

"Babe, you don't need to fix shit. It's only burnt eggs, not a big deal," Josh says as he runs water over the frying pan.

"I can fix it. It's okay. It'll be okay." I keep repeating the mantra in my head. If I say it enough times, it might be true.

Josh comes up and shuts the fridge. He pulls my body tight to his as his arms wrap around me. "Emmy, it's okay. It's just burnt eggs. It doesn't matter. You're okay. I'm okay. We are okay." He kisses the top of my head.

My fingers curl around the lapels of his jacket. I don't want him to let me go. I want everything he says to be real. I want us to be okay, even though I know we never will be. We have an expiration date. He just doesn't know it yet.

"You need to get out of your head, Em. I'm not him. I'm an asshole. I'm not going to pretend that I'm not. But I'm not the monster haunting your dreams. There is nothing you can do that will ever make me want to hurt you."

"I know that. Deep down, I do know that. I just can't help the constant feeling that I'm going to do something wrong. I'm not the same girl you knew in high school, remember, Josh?"

"Of course you're not the same. You're better. You're more real now than you ever let yourself be back then. I don't need a fake, plastered smile on your lips constantly, Emmy. I'd love nothing more than to always see genuine happiness written all over your face. But I love you no matter what you're feeling. When you're scared, I still love you. I want to hold you and make you feel safe. I want to slay every mother-fucking demon you have that makes you scared. If you're angry, I still love you. I may want to throw you down on the bed and fuck the shit out of you, because, damn, babe, you're fucking hot as hell when you get fired up. Don't even get me started on when you're jealous. If you're sad, I still love you. I want to be the one to wipe your tears away. I want to be the shoulder you cry on."

I don't know how to respond to any of that. This Josh… This fierce, overbearing, protective Josh… This is the one I fell in love with when I was just fifteen. It's twisted and fucked up, I know. After all the shit he did in high school, after taking my virginity and warning me to leave town the next day, I should hate him. I try to remind myself I hate him. But the truth is, as much as I want to, I can't.

No one has ever loved me the way he does, even if it is a little crazy. Okay, *a lot crazy*. But I've never felt safer than I do right now, in his arms.

"Some days I really hate you; I remember waking up alone in that cabin and I hate you. But most days, even on the worst days of my life, all I wanted was to be held by you."

"Why didn't you call me sooner, Emmy? I would have come for you."

"I know you would have—that's why I never called. I knew what you would do. I don't want you to get in trouble over me, Josh."

"There is no amount of trouble you're not worth," he says as a ping sounds through the room.

Then I hear the clicking of heels on the marble floor and I step back. My body tightens. Please don't let it be another one of Josh's *friends*. I don't think I can handle that.

"Josh, why do I have two men, who look like they just stepped out of the WWE, following me up here?" Ella's voice carries through the house.

I raise my eyebrows at Josh in question. He laughs as he grabs my hand, leading me out of the kitchen. I've never really felt too self-conscious when I'm around Josh. But right now, with how glamourous Ella is in her skin-tight, little black dress and red pumps—her hair falling down over her shoulders in

thick dark waves and red lipstick painted on her lips
—I can't help but think she looks like a goddess. And
all I want to do is crawl under a rock and never come
back out.

"What the fuck, Ella? Does Dean know you left the
house looking like that?" Josh asks.

"Don't be stupid. Of course he doesn't know. He
wasn't exactly invited to our little shopping trip, which,
by the way, I'm going to need one of your fancy
McKinley money credit cards." Ella holds her hand out.

"Hasn't anyone told you?" Josh asks as he digs out
his wallet, removing yet another black card and
handing it over to her without question.

"Told me what?"

"That you are a McKinley. I happen to know you
have a card with the name Ella McKinley on it. I
ordered it myself."

"Well, yeah, but it's more fun to spend *your* money."

"It all comes from the same place, Ella," Josh says.
"Also, change of plans. Emily's not feeling up to going
out in the city. She's going to use the computer in the
study and do some online shopping."

Ella looks directly at me and smiles. "Emily, blink
once if you need help. Twice, if you want me to knock
this one on his ass. I've done it before."

My eyes open in surprise—surely she can't actually
put him on his ass. "Ah, I'm okay. I just don't feel like
going out. I'm sorry for interrupting your day." My
hands wring the fabric on the bottom of my shirt.

Josh takes hold of one of them. "Emily, this is Ben

and Jacob. They'll be your security detail whenever I'm not here."

I glance over to the two hulking men in suits. They don't say anything. They just stand there, looking scary.

I hold Josh's hand tighter. He's not actually going to leave me here with the two of them, is he? Ella must notice my distress and she speaks up.

"Josh, they are not hanging out inside the apartment. I'm inviting my sisters over, and we're having a girls' day. Your wrestlers can serve and protect from downstairs."

"Okay, but Reilly is not helping Emily buy clothes." Josh agrees to have the men wait in the lobby.

He cups my face between his hands and slowly brings his lips down onto mine. The moment our mouths touch, I forget that we're not alone in the room. Everything else drains out, everything but the feel of his lips on me.

The kiss ends way too soon for my liking. I cling to the lapels of his jacket tighter. I'm not sure I want him to leave. Maybe I should go with him. No, my mind is such a mess right now. Some distance will be good.

"You okay?" Josh asks.

"Yeah, I'm fine," I answer. "You are coming back, right?" I ask. What if this is one of his cruel, twisted games from the past and he's going to leave me here?

"Emmy, I promise there is nothing that will keep me from coming back to you." He kisses me again. Leaning down, he whispers in my ear, "There's a phone in the bedroom drawer for you—use it if you need me. My number's saved. There's also a gun placed in that drawer, one in the top left drawer in the kitchen, one in my study under my desk, one in the lounge room under the coffee table and another in the entry table, middle drawer. Shoot first, ask questions later if you have to." He winks at me as he backs away, my eyes wide. Why the hell does he have so many guns in the house?

CHAPTER TWELVE

JOSH

*T*he whole way down the elevator, through the lobby and getting to the car, I fight everything in me not to turn around and go back to Emmy. As soon as I get in the car, I pull out my phone and press the number I've stored for Emmy. It rings out. Fuck, I told her there was a phone in the bedroom if *she* needed to call *me*, not the other way around.

I dial Ella's number instead. The call almost rings out before she answers. I was prepared to jump out of the car and run back upstairs.

"Did you forget something?" she answers in a singsong voice.

"Put Emily on the phone," I grunt out.

"What if she doesn't want to speak to you right now? Let me check." Ella laughs.

"Emily, there is one overbearing asshole with separation issues on the phone and wanting to speak with you," Ella says to Emmy.

"What?" Emily asks, and the moment I hear her voice, my muscles begin to relax.

"Josh is on the phone. You want me to hang up?" Ella asks her.

"Don't you dare fucking hang up on me, Ella," I yell loudly. I know she hears me when she laughs.

"It's okay," Emily says tentatively. Seconds later, she's speaking into the phone.

"Josh, are you okay?" she asks.

"I am now," I breathe out.

"Okay." She waits for me to say something else. I don't care how crazy I look or sound when I'm around Emily. She's seen me at my worst and loves me anyway. Even though she hasn't said those words back to me yet, I know her heart.

"Emmy, I need you to go into our bedroom for me," I instruct her.

"Sure, hold on," she says. "Okay, I'm in the room."

"Open the top bedside drawer and take out the phone that's in there." I wait for her to follow the instruction.

"Okay, got it."

"Now turn it on."

"It's turning on. Are you sure you're okay? You don't sound like you are."

"I didn't know it would be this hard," I admit.

"What would be?"

"Leaving you in the apartment, being away from you, not being right next to you."

"Yeah, I know…"

"I want you to keep that phone on you. Text me, call me, send me pictures throughout the day. Please." I'm practically begging for any morsel of attention she'll throw my way.

"You want me to send you pictures… what of?" She laughs.

"Your face. I miss seeing it already."

"Okay, let me figure out how to work this fancy phone first. I haven't…" Her sentence cuts off.

"You haven't what, Emmy?" I urge her to continue.

"I, um… haven't had a phone for a while so I'm a little out of touch, that's all."

"How long is a while?" I ask. The more info I can get, the more I can use it to find out who (or what) she's running from.

"Three years," she answers.

"Fuck!" My fingers grip the phone so tight I'm surprised it's not crumbling in my hands. Three fucking years! She's been living under someone else's control for three fucking years. She's been beaten and abused and God only knows what for three fucking years.

"Josh?" Emmy's voice is strained. It took a lot for her to tell me that little bit of information, and I've just yelled my frustration through the phone.

"I had a dream last night, babe," I tell her. It's a lie,

but I need to change the topic. I need to reassure her that she's okay. That she's safe.

"You had a dream? Okay, what about?" she asks.

"You were riding Jasper. You were wearing these little denim shorts and a white top. Tan boots. Your hair was blowing in the wind behind you. Fuck, now I'm hard again, picturing that image of you in my head."

"Me, on a horse, turns you on? That's... *strange*, Josh, even for you," she says.

"*You* turn me on, Emmy. But that dream, I want to see it. Make sure you buy those tiny shorts and boots today."

"Sure. How long do you have to be at the office?" she asks, her voice quiet.

"I'm going to be in and out. I'll be back before you know it. Unless you want me to turn the car around and come back now?" Part of me is begging for her to say yes. To give me any reason to go back to her.

"No, it's okay. I think it might be fun to hang out with Ella and her sisters."

"Emmy, remember, it's your home. You can kick them out whenever you've had enough of them. You don't owe anyone anything," I tell her.

"It's your house, Josh, and I'm not about to kick your family out of it."

"It's *ours*. And the only one who is family is Ella. The other two are her family, not ours. The redheaded one is batshit crazy. Don't let her choose clothes for you."

"Okay."

I know I need to hang up, but I don't want to. I don't think she wants to either.

"I gotta go. I love you, Emmy. Don't ever forget that." My voice chokes with emotions I'm not used to feeling.

"I know," she replies.

"I know too, babe," I tell her; she doesn't have to say it back. I know she will when she's ready.

I'M annoyed as fuck the moment I walk through the office. "Mr. McKinley, good to see you back, sir," Kathy, my sixty-year-old assistant, says from her desk outside my door.

"Kathy, what am I in for today?" I ask her. If anyone knows what's going on in this building, it's her.

"We have you until two. You have a meeting with the board at ten, a lunch meeting with Hunter Jackson from Jackson Imports, and then a meeting with the legal department at one thirty."

"What the fuck does the legal department want?" I ask. They're not the ones who usually call for meetings.

"Something about your brother getting married without a prenup. The board isn't too happy about that either." She smiles.

"Well, the board can kiss my ass. Ella is now a McKinley; she's entitled to the shares that are being transferred into her name. I want to make sure she's protected if anything were to happen to Dean," I tell her. "Besides, they should be more concerned over the fact that *I* fully intend on getting married without a fucking prenup."

The thought leaves my lips, then my words sink in. Did I just say I'm getting married? Kathy's eyes widen and a huge smile spreads across her face.

"Did you meet someone? Who is she?" she asks.

I don't answer her. Shaking my head, I storm into my office. My love life is not going to be the fucking talk around the water cooler. Sitting down at my desk, I send a text to Emily.

Me: Did you buy those shorts yet?

Emmy: Not yet. Ella says I need to buy out the whole store of some place called La Perla. Don't worry, I told her I'm doing no such thing.

La Perla, I know exactly what that is. And I fucking approve. Fuck, I'll buy the fucking franchise if it means I get to see Emily in all of that shit.

Me: Yes, you are! Get clicking, babe. One in every style, every colour. I want to see the fucking rainbow on you!

Emmy: I'll check it out.

Me: I gotta go, but if you don't shop up big there, I'll just go there myself and buy everything.

Emmy: Don't work too hard. XX

Checking the time, I have ten minutes until this fucking board meeting. I need to catch up with Sam before I go in there. Stopping in his office doorway, I see him hitting at the keyboard on his desk.

"What did that keyboard ever do to you?" I ask.

He doesn't stop, totally ignoring my comment instead. A minute later, he smiles. "Gotcha, mother-fucker!" he shouts.

I raise my eyebrows in question. It's not unusual for Sam to get animated or excited when he finally manages to get into something he was being kept out of.

"I have the name of the fucker who registered both death certificates." He smiles at me.

"And that is?"

"Gregory Jones. Detective Gregory Jones," Sam says, picking up a pile of files and walking towards the door.

"Who the fuck is Gregory Jones, and what the fuck does he have to do with Emily?" I ask aloud.

"No idea. *Yet*," he replies. "Try not to kill off any of the board members," Sam adds as we walk into the boardroom.

The room falls into silence as I take a seat at the head of the table. I've always fucking hated these meetings. They're full of stuffy, old, overweight men. Men just like my fucking father.

It was supposed to be Dean in this seat, not me. He never worked a day in his life in this company—my father gave up trying to mould him. Instead, the son of a bitch focused all his energy on me, making me the next head of McKinley Industries.

Let's just say, he's not a man who's missed by anyone. The only reason I gave Emily up when we were kids was because I was so afraid I would turn out like my father. An abusive, entitled asshole. I didn't want to ever put that on Emily.

My hands clench on the desk as I think about the three years of abuse she's endured anyway. Three years I could have saved her from... I *should have* saved her from. Whoever made up that shit about if you love someone let them go is a goddamn fucking idiot. If you love someone, the only way to keep them safe is to fucking keep them in the first place.

"Mr. McKinley, we're ready whenever you are, sir," Sam says from next to me. The sooner we get this shit-show over with, the sooner I get back to Emily. I nod my head, indicating that I'm listening—even if I'm only half paying attention.

IT'S one in the afternoon by the time I get five minutes to myself. I send Emily a quick text to check in, something I've wanted to do for a while.

Me: How are you?

Emmy: Reallllly goooood. How you doinnn?????

Her reply comes in quick, almost like she was watching the phone for it to ring, although I'm not sure what to make of her message.

Me: I'd be better if I was home with you. What are you up to?

Emmy: I'd be better if you were in me too.

Great, now I have a fucking boner. I'm sitting in the car heading back to the office with a fucking boner.

Emmy: With. Not in. Although, now that I think about it...

I don't bother to text back. I dial her number. She picks up straight away.

"Hellooooo," she sings.

"Babe, what are you doing?"

"Um, well, Ella's sisters are here and they made these drinks. I didn't want to be rude so I drank some. And now I feel good. Like really good, Josh. But not as good as you make me feel," she slurs.

"Are you drunk?" I ask, already knowing the answer.

"Um, I don't know. Hold on," she says. I don't think she pulls the phone away from her ear as she speaks to Ella.

"Ella, Joshua is asking if I'm drunk. Am I drunk?" she asks. I hear a heap of laughter before some shuffling of the phone.

"Joshy, she's not drunk. *Much*. Where are you anyway? You're missing the fun," Ella says.

"Ella, what are you drinking? What is Emmy drinking? Has she eaten? Had any water?" I fire off. The only response I get is more laughter.

"Give the phone back to Emily," I growl out.

"Joshua, remember that time in high school when you took me home from that party?" Emmy asks.

I'm surprised she remembers that; she was out of it. She passed out in my car. I don't know how much or what she was drinking at the party, but when I turned up and saw how wasted she was, I dragged her ass out.

"You remember that?" I ask her

"Yep!" She pops out the P sound. "I wasn't drunk that night. I faked it because I knew you'd take me home. It was the first time you told me that you loved me."

"You were supposed to be asleep when I said that."

"I know. But I'm not faking drunk now. So, you know, if you want to tell me now, that's okay too," she says, not making any sense.

"I love you, Emmy. Have you eaten anything today?"

"Mmm," she hums.

"Emmy?"

"Oh, hang on." She returns her attention to the girls. "I lick, drink then suck, right?" she asks.

Fuck me, they're giving her tequila shots. I hear a bunch of females cheering before Emmy starts talking again.

"I don't get it... it tastes like shit, Josh. Why do people do this?"

"Emmy, drink some water, babe. I'm coming home," I tell her.

"Oh, can we do that thing again?" she asks.

"What thing?"

"You know that thing you do with your tongue. Down there," she attempts to whisper.

"Babe, I will be doing that thing with my tongue on a daily basis. Don't you worry about that."

I can hear giggles and wolf whistles in the background.

"Emmy, I'm hanging up now. I'm coming home."

"Josh, are you mad? I don't want you to be mad at me."

"I'm not mad. I just really miss you, that's all."

"Yeah, I miss you too. The girls want to go to some place called The Merge. But I don't want to go, Josh. What if they find me there?" she says.

I pause. "Emmy, who? What if who finds you?" I prompt, hoping like fuck that she's drunk enough to let something slip.

I hear a bang. "Emmy, Emmy?" I yell through the receiver.

"Oopsie-daisy. I dropped the phone, but don't worry, it's not broken or anything," she says before she starts rambling on again, "Josh, my lips are numb, but I really want you to kiss them. I like your kisses. They're nice."

I laugh. I like drunk Emmy. I need to call my brother though, which means I need to hang up the phone.

"Emmy, babe, have those lips ready for me. I plan on kissing the hell out of them as soon as I get home."

"Well, hurry up then," she says before the phone cuts out.

I dial Dean straight away.

"Yeah?" he answers.

"Your wife is currently in my apartment giving Emily tequila shots," I grunt.

"Last I checked Emily was an adult?" he replies.

"I currently have four drunk women in my penthouse, Dean. Three too many. Come and fucking get them."

"What do you mean four? Who else is there?"

"Ella, Reilly and Alyssa."

"Fucking hell. I thought Ella was taking Emily shopping."

"Emily wanted to shop online. I don't know how the others got involved. But you need to come and get them."

"Okay, Zac and I are on our way."

I hang up as I pull up out front of the building.

CHAPTER THIRTEEN

EMILY

*M*y head is spinning. This tequila is really good stuff. As soon as I hear the ping of the elevator, I get up and run to the foyer (at least I try to run). I stumble my way through the penthouse. The moment I see Josh, or two of him, I jump up, wrapping my legs around his waist.

My lips find his, my tongue pushing its way inside his mouth, not that he puts up any resistance. Before I know it, he's got me pinned up against the wall. He takes control over the kiss, tilting my head to give him better access. I can feel his hardness against my centre, every movement of his hips sending me further and further into a frenzy.

Josh slows down the kiss, before pulling away. "Miss me?" he asks.

"You were gone a really, really long time," I tell him with a pout.

"I know."

"Emily, it's your turn!" Ella shouts from the living room.

"Oh, it's my turn. Put me down. Put me down. It's my turn." I unwrap my legs from his waist, my feet landing on the floor. Josh doesn't let go. His arms hold me close as I struggle to keep myself upright.

Once I've got myself steady, I look up at him. "It's my turn. Let's go."

"It's your turn for what?" he asks as he holds me still.

"Our game. Come see." I unlatch his arms and drag him by the hand through to the living room, where the three girls are waiting for me.

"About time, I was about to take your turn," Ella says.

"Damn, Josh, who knew you'd clean up so well." Reilly whistles. I glare at her. It's just like high school, when all the hot girls would be pining for Josh to give them some attention.

Josh ignores her. Instead, he wraps his arm around my shoulder, pulling me into his chest. "Mmm, you smell good. Why do you smell good?" I ask him.

"Because I showered?" he questions back.

I shrug. I don't really care why he smells good, as long as I can stay tucked up in here and sniff him.

"Gross, Emily, it's your turn. Hurry up and get that little ass of yours down here," Ella squeals.

I take my seat next to her. "Okay, sorry, but I'm not really sorry. He has a really good tongue," I whisper back to her.

"So does his brother." Ella winks at me and I laugh.

I lick my hand and hold it out. Ella sprinkles the salt on it. "Oh, wait! I have a better idea. Josh, get over here, and lose the shirt."

Josh raises his eyebrows at me. "Lose the shirt? Why?" he asks as he strips his jacket off and loosens his tie.

"I want to lick you," I say simply. All the girls start laughing, and I join in with them. "If you knew how good he tasted, you'd want to lick him too." I point to each of them.

"Trust me, Emily, we do not want to know. Besides, nothing tastes as good as Zac," Alyssa says.

"My husband has a pierced cucumber. And when you lick it…" Reilly laughs.

"Argh, God. Josh, shoot me now," Ella grumbles.

Josh squats down behind me, picking me up before placing me in his lap. His arms close around my waist. "Sorry, El, I happen to like you, which is rare, so you're not getting shot." He lifts up my tequila and downs it in one go.

"Hey, not fair. That was mine," I complain.

"Okay, where're you licking, babe?" Josh asks as he undoes the first few buttons of his shirt.

"Really, I can lick you?" I'm so excited. I jump up and down. Josh's hands go to my waist, stilling my movements.

"Anytime, anywhere," he says.

I pull his shirt off his shoulder a little and lick a spot at his neck. "Salt," I say, holding my hand out. Ella places the salt in my open palm.

I pour it over Josh's neck. "Okay, where's my shot?" Josh hands me a glass. Then he places a slice of lemon between his teeth.

I don't waste time. I lick, drink and suck on that lemon. It tastes gross. My nose scrunches up. "Ugh, I don't know why people like this stuff."

"Have any of you had water since you turned my living room into a bar?" Josh asks. Why is he suddenly sounding like the responsible one?

I look around. "Water? Yep, it's clear, just like water." I point to the three bottles of tequila that are on the table. They're all open and half empty.

Josh looks at the bottles. "Wait, is that my...? Fucking hell. Ella, did you raid my bar or did you bring these supplies with you?" he asks her, nodding to the table.

"*Yours*. You have the good stuff too, you know." Ella smiles.

"You do know that's a two-thousand-dollar bottle you're spilling all over my damn table? I'm sending your husband the bill," Josh says to Ella.

I, on the other hand, just about choke. I've been drinking a two-thousand-dollar bottle of tequila. Who the hell pays that much for one little bottle?

"Alyssa, you look the most responsible. Can you

please go get some water bottles from the fridge?" Josh asks.

"Sure," she says, as she goes to stand up and starts tumbling.

"Fuck me, you're all as bad as each other. Alyssa, sit your ass down. I'll get you water."

"Oh, pizza, that's a great idea, Josh. I'll have a meat lovers," Reilly squeals.

"Yes. Pizza, pizza, pizza!" Ella starts cheering.

I can't remember the last time I ate pizza. Do I even still like it?

"Pizza actually is a fucking fantastic idea. Let me order some. What kind do you want, Emmy?" Josh asks me.

It seems like everyone's eyes go to me. "I don't mind. Whatever you all want is fine," I say.

"Chicken, no, cheese. Oh, pepperoni!" Ella says.

"Okay, I've got this. Emmy, help me in the kitchen." Josh stands, picking me up with him.

"Oh, *help*. Is that what the kids are calling it these days!" Ella winks. All three women burst into laughter.

"Where's Zac, because I could really use his *help* right now." Alyssa giggles.

"Gross, no. Josh, wait for me. I'm coming." Ella goes to stand up but wobbles so much she falls back down in a fit of laughter.

"Fuck my life. Change of plans." Josh pulls his phone out of his pocket and presses some buttons, before sitting back down.

"Where the fuck are you?" he yells through the receiver.

"Almost there. Why?" A rough voice comes over the speaker.

"Oh, Dean, hunny, are you coming to *help* me? 'Cause I really need *help!*" Ella yells. We all burst into laughter with her.

"How much has she had to drink?" Dean asks.

"I don't fucking know, but they're all fucking drunk as skunks. Hurry up and get your ass here. And bring pizza. They want pizza."

"Do I look like a delivery boy?" Dean says.

Josh holds the phone out in Ella's direction. "El, tell Dean to bring pizza."

"Oh, yes, pizza!" Everyone starts shouting.

Josh hangs up the phone and throws it on the table.

"Josh, your brother's a little scary," I tell him.

"You're scared of Dean? When you sleep next to *that one* at night?" Reilly asks me.

"That one? You mean Josh? He's not scary at all. Are you, Josh?" I turn into him.

"No, babe, not at all. Remember that." He kisses my forehead, and I melt into him.

ARGH, God, why is my head pounding? I feel a body move behind me and I tense up. What did I do last night? I don't remember what I did to make him mad. I try to catalogue my other injuries. But all I feel is nausea. I need to find the bathroom. I climb out of bed as quietly as I can. Nothing other than my head hurts, so maybe it's not that bad.

Although it must have been a pretty big hit, for me to feel this nauseous. This doesn't happen that often. But when it does, it can last for days.

I find the bathroom, my stomach emptying as soon as I'm near the loo. My head pounds as I lean back against the wall and close my eyes.

"Babe, here, drink some of this."

I must be dreaming because I just heard Josh's voice. It's times like these that I wish I could go to him. I wish I could take the phone out of the cistern and call him. Why can't I just call him?

"Emmy, open your eyes. You need to drink a little," he says.

"If I open my eyes, you'll be gone, and I'll be back in hell. Just let me dream a little longer," I whisper. I cannot let Trent know I'm awake. I don't have the energy to deal with him yet.

"Emmy, I'm right here. I'm not going anywhere. Open your eyes, babe." I feel his hands place a bottle in mine. That feels a little too real. I jolt back, my eyes springing open.

"Josh?" I ask. How did he find me? "How... how did you find me?" I say the question aloud this time.

"Emmy, you're okay. Look around. You're not there anymore." He scoops me up and carries me back to bed. The room I'm in... it's not where I thought I was.

I'm in Josh's apartment. The last few days come back to me. Mostly.

"Why does my head hurt so much?" I ask him.

"Tequila. You and Ella both finished off the bottle." Josh hands me two pills. "Take these. This is just ibuprofen—it'll help with the headache. And this one's for the nausea."

"I think I'm dying," I complain. I don't handle being sick well at all. Now that my heart has calmed down a bit, blurry parts of last night are coming back to me.

"You're not dying. You're just hungover. Haven't you ever been hungover before?" he asks.

"No, I wasn't allowed." I shut my mouth, choosing to shove the pills into it instead. I'm obviously getting way too comfortable around Josh for me to keep slipping up like this. He doesn't need to know about the last few years of my life. The less he knows, the better.

"Argh, why didn't you stop me?" I groan as I lie back down and snuggle into the blanket.

"You were having fun. You're also a full-grown adult, Emmy. If you want to let loose and blow off steam, I'm not about to stop you."

I think about what he said. He's not about to stop me. I wonder if he'd stop me if I was to get up and walk out the door now? The only problem is, I'm too scared to test the theory. What if he didn't stop me? I don't know if I want to leave this dream yet.

I watch as he pulls on a pair of grey sweats. God, what is it with this man and grey sweatpants? How many pairs can one person have? He comes over to the bed, leans down and kisses my forehead while stroking his hand through my hair.

"I promised Ella I'd meet her for breakfast. Do you want to get up and come eat?"

I shake my head, which was a mistake. "Argh, no. I'm just going to stay right here."

"I doubt Ella is actually awake anyway. I'm going to bring you back some food." He gets up and walks to the door.

"Josh?"

He turns and looks at me, waiting for me to speak up. I get a little lost in all of the tanned muscles and ink currently on display on his bare chest.

"Need something, Emmy?" He smirks.

"No, but you need a damn shirt. And don't you have any other colour sweatpants than grey?" I ask.

"No, I like grey. But I will put a shirt on. For you." He walks into the closet and comes back out with a tight white V-neck on. Is he purposely messing with me?

"Better?" he asks.

"Not at all," I grumble and roll over. I hear him laugh as he walks out the door.

▽

"No, stop. Trent, stop. Please, I didn't mean to. I'll fix it," I beg him. He doesn't listen.

"You fucking stupid whore. How fucking hard is it to

place the damn towels on the towel rail. Look at them." He *shoves my head into the rail.*

I hear the crunch of bone, a searing pain tearing at my face. I scream. Blood pours out of my nose.

Trent lets go of the hold he has on my hair and I fall to the floor, landing on my hands and knees.

"Now you've gone and made a bigger fucking mess. The shit better be fucking cleaned up when I get back." I see his booted foot come for my head. I scream.

I jolt up in the bed. Someone is screaming. Who's screaming? The door bursts open and Josh runs in, holding a gun directly at me. Dean comes in after him. Both men stop when they see me. Josh scans the room quickly then lowers the firearm, his jaw tense.

"Fuck!" Josh screams. He turns and punches the wall behind him, not just once but three times.

"Josh, calm the fuck down, *now,*" Dean growls.

I just sit in the middle of the bed, watching. Waiting. I don't know exactly what I'm waiting for, but I'm waiting. Josh places the gun down on the dresser. His icy blue eyes stare, meeting mine.

I've made him angry again. All I ever seem to do is make people angry. I don't know what to say, what to do, so I just sit and wait.

"Emily, are you okay?" Dean asks me. I nod my head, but I don't take my eyes off Josh.

"Good. Joshua, a word." Dean walks out of the room. I think that Josh is going to follow his brother, but when he gets to the door, he slams it shut and locks it instead. He bangs his forehead on it a few times before turning back around and heading to the bed.

I should be looking for a way to get out of here. Any normal person would not want to be alone in a locked room with Josh right now. He's acting like a caged lion, ready to rip the head off anyone who's close. I'd be lying if I said I wasn't a little unsure. *Not scared.* I've never been truly scared of Josh, but *unsure.*

I'm unsure of what's going through his head. I'm unsure of what I should be doing to help him.

"Josh, I need you to tell me what to do. I don't know what I'm supposed to do." I'm trying to not let the tears fall—trying and failing miserably.

Josh comes and sits on the bed, pulling me into his lap. He brushes the sweaty hair out of my face. I still slightly flinch when his hand reaches up. He doesn't mention my reaction, just continues to brush the hair off my face.

"You don't have to do anything, Emmy. You aren't meant to do anything. I'm sorry if I scared you. I'm sorry. I'm so fucking sorry that I can't slay the demons that haunt you in your sleep."

"It's not your fault," I tell him.

"It is. If I didn't make you leave, if I had just kept you back then…" His words trail off but I know what he doesn't say.

How can he possibly think any of this is his fault? This is my fault. I should have been smarter, gotten out sooner.

"Josh, it's not your fault. Whatever choices were

161

made, I made them, not you." I take hold of his hands. "Can we go back to the farm?" I ask, wanting to change the subject, and maybe distract him from his own thoughts.

"Yeah, let's shower then we'll head back." Right as we are about to get up, the door opens.

"What the fuck! Josh, out. Emily and I are having a girls' morning. We will accept a delivery of mimosas." Ella comes barrelling in with her hands full of bags.

"How the fuck did you even get in here?" Josh asks, making no move to get out.

"I picked the lock. Bray taught me how when we were kids. Never really thought I'd be thankful for those painful hours. But here we are." She drops the bags on the bed.

"Babe, want me to send her back to the loony bin she came from?" Josh asks me.

I shake my head no. "No, I want to keep her," I tell him.

He smiles. "Okay, I'll bring you back some food, and mimosas, *and water*."

AFTER WHAT FEELS like hours of being primped and prodded, Ella declares that we're ready.

"Are you sure about this, Ella? We're only going to be spending a few hours in a car heading back to the farm. This is too much."

I stare at my reflection in the mirror. Ella gave me a

royal blue dress; it's made of a light, sheer material. The dress has thin spaghetti straps that crisscross at the back, with a deep V-cut along the neckline that shows off way too much cleavage. The fabric falls halfway down my thighs, so although it's not that short, it feels short. So much of my skin is showing.

Ella put soft curls in my hair, leaving them hanging down my back. It's my face that has me most confused. I don't recognise the woman staring back at me. All the fading yellow bruising has been covered over and hidden under the flawless makeup Ella applied. Shiny pink lips and dark eyeliner make my blue eyes appear bigger than I've ever seen them look.

"You're stunning, Emily. Josh is going to be tripping over his own tongue. I can't wait. Come on, let's go. Remember, confidence. You are a strong, confident woman, and no one, not even Josh, is going to be telling you what to wear." Ella's pep talk hits me harder than it should.

I can't bring myself to tell her how wrong she is. I'm not strong or confident. And honestly, if Josh hates the dress and wants me to change, I'm probably not going to argue with him about it. As much as I want to have Ella's confidence and self-esteem, I just don't. What I *can do* is fake it for a little while.

"Okay, let's go."

CHAPTER FOURTEEN

JOSH

*E*mmy's been holed up in the bedroom with Ella for two hours. What the fuck could they possibly be doing that takes two hours? I've attempted to go in a few times, only to be screamed at by Ella telling me to get out.

I've tried to distract myself, going through emails and boring-ass reports for work, but every few minutes, I'm pulled back to the image of Emmy sitting up in the bed, screaming at the top of her lungs with tears running down her face.

I'm such a fucking idiot for not controlling my reactions better. I should have been able to keep my cool. I'm surprised she's not running for the hills with how I acted, unless she's too scared to try. Fuck, is she only here because she's too scared of what I'll do if she tries to leave? I did tell her I'm not about to let her go.

And I'm fucking not, but I also would not hurt her either. I'll do anything to keep her. I'll also do anything to make her nightmares disappear. Dragging my fingers through my hair, I can't help but think how much I'd fucking love a drink right now. But I'm refraining. I need to be as clear-minded as I can be. I need to figure the fuck out who did this to Emmy, who the fuck is continuing to haunt her.

"You look like shit," Dean says as he walks in with two large coffee cups.

"Thank you, I do try hard," I remark.

"Here, drink this. Are you sure you're going to be okay?" he pries.

"I'm fine. I just need to find the fucker who did this to her."

"I get that, I do. But I worry about you. With her, it's different. Your obsession with her has already been a little much. But now that she's back, it's off the fucking charts—hospital territory," Dean says.

"Yeah, how's that differ from your obsession with Ella?" I ask him.

"If Ella wanted to walk out that door without me, I'd probably let her. Can you say the same?"

"Fuck no. But I also don't care. I let her go once, and look what happened to her."

"Josh, whatever happened to her is not on you. It's on the fucker who did it. Not you."

"I always thought if I kept her around, I'd end up

like him. Like dad. That's why I sent her away. Guess the joke's on me because the life I thought I was saving her from, she ended up having anyway."

"You are not like him. Never have been. Do you think I'd leave you alone with Ella, even for a minute, if you were? Fuck that. He does not define who you are."

Dean gets worked up whenever the topic of our asshole father comes up. I don't actually know why, but he hates him more than I do. And from what I remember, Dean hardly had anything to do with him at all in the later years. No, that shit was all left up to me.

"I know that now, but when I was eighteen, I obviously wasn't as smart." I sip at the coffee; it's burnt and fucking disgusting, but I drink it anyway. "How much longer do you think they're going to be?" I ask, looking at my watch.

"Your guess is as good as mine." Just as he sits across from me, I hear the sound of Ella and Emmy laughing as they come down the hall.

I'm too impatient to wait for her. I get up and meet her just as she's about to enter the living room. The moment my eyes land on her, I'm speechless. Fuck me, Emmy is always beautiful. But right now, fuck, she's fucking gorgeous.

My eyes travel up and down her body numerous times. I wouldn't be surprised if I was drooling right now. I have an instant fucking boner.

Emmy stands still, wringing her hands in front of her. "If you don't like it, I can change," she says.

If I don't like it? Is she blind? The only reason that

dress is coming off her is because I'm ripping it off to worship the body underneath it.

"Emmy, do you like the dress?" I ask her.

"I like it." She smiles at me.

"So, keep it on then. You look fucking gorgeous, babe," I tell her as I pull her close to me. I don't think I can ever get enough of her being in my arms. "Are you ready to head back?"

"More than ready," she says.

"Oh, Dean, I'm heading up to the farm with Emily and Josh for a few days," Ella adds in. That's news to me.

"Why?" Dean and I both ask at the same time.

"Because your mum invited me. She said something about wedding planning."

"Okay, I'll come down tomorrow. I need to sort some things out here first." Dean picks Ella up off the ground, kissing her.

Yep, don't need to see that shit. I'm surprised he's not insisting on coming down today with her. I do suspect he'll be there before midnight. There's no way he's going all night without Ella attached to him.

"Okay, we'll be downstairs. Car's leaving in five minutes, El, with or without you," I tell her as I lead Emmy to the elevator.

▽

NEVER AGAIN! Never fucking again will I take a fucking three-hour road trip with both Ella and Emily together. If I didn't already have shares in a parac-etamol company, I'm about to fucking buy some.

Nonstop talking and laughing the whole trip. Add in the off-key singing and you have yourself a fucking migraine. The only reason I didn't tell them both to shut the fuck up was because of how happy Emily was. Hearing her laugh and be carefree is what I imagine angels sound like.

Not that I'm ever going to meet any angels, other than Emily. I'm sure if there is a maker up there somewhere, he'd be chewing someone's ass out for their mistake of making Emily and me soulmates. Her pureness should never have gotten mixed up with my level of evil.

Too late now, motherfuckers. She's mine and I don't give a fuck what anyone has to say about it. Pulling up in front of the house, I glare at the fucker who is about to open Emily's door for her. He quickly walks around the car, choosing to open Ella's instead. I know he's doing the job I fucking pay him to do, but I want to be the one opening doors for her, not any other fuckers.

"Thank you." Emily smiles at me as she climbs out of the car.

"Anytime." I smirk. Taking her hand, I lead her inside with Ella following behind.

"Shit, I probably should have thought about this whole night without Dean thing a little better," she says.

"You'll be fine. It's one night, El," I tell her.

"Sure, I'll be fine. It's only one night," she repeats.

Something is off with her now that we're here. I don't like it. I don't like the way she's withdrawing into herself. I've seen her do it a few times before. I've seen the way she rubs at her wrists, and I've seen the scars she tries to cover up.

"Babe, can you take this to my office for me? I'm just going to grab a drink, then I've got a few things I need to catch up on. I thought you and Ella could hang out a bit while I work." I hand over my laptop bag to Emily.

If only she knew how much trust I'm putting in her hands right now. I don't let anyone touch that laptop. There is access to literally billions of dollars on that one machine. Emily looks between Ella and me before nodding her head.

"Sure, how about I have a quick shower and meet you at the pool?" she asks Ella.

"Yeah, sounds good," Ella responds, a little vacant. Emily's eyebrows draw down, but she silently turns around and heads towards my office.

I wait for her to be out of earshot before I speak to Ella.

"What's wrong? And don't fucking try to lie to me. I already know your tells. You can't lie for shit."

"Nothing's wrong. I just don't know how I'm going to get through a whole night without Dean. I mean, if you were having sex with him, you'd understand what that man can do." She smirks.

"Try again," I say.

"I… okay, I don't know. What if I can't do it? What if I get that urge to…?" Her sentence trails off.

"Then you come to me, Ella."

"You don't know, Josh. You don't know what I do," she says quietly, averting her eyes as if she's ashamed.

"El, you don't have anything to be ashamed of. And you don't need to say it either. *I know*." I hold her wrist, turning it over. "These scars do not define who you are. They are a part of you, not the whole you. Do you know who you are, Ella?"

"Who am I?" she asks.

"You're Ella fucking McKinley. The McKinley Princess is what they're calling you in the papers. Hold your head up high. You don't bow down to any mother-fuckers. You make them bow down to you."

"Okay, thank you," she says as she's about to walk away.

"Ella, I may not be Dean or Bray. But I know better than anyone about battling internal demons. If you need to talk, you come to me."

"Thank you." She heads for the stairs.

When I walk into the office, Emily is sitting at my desk typing on my laptop. She's so focused on what she's looking at, or for, that she doesn't notice I'm there. I wait, giving her more time. More time to search for whatever it is she felt the need to hack into my computer for. Not that it would have been hard— the password is *Emmy*. She would have guessed that right away.

I'm surprised I'm not more furious about the fact

that she's on my computer. Anyone else would have a bullet between their eyes right now. But with Emily, I'm more intrigued to find out what she's looking for. She doesn't realise this, but that computer has software that tracks every single keystroke. Even if she tried to delete what she's searching for, she won't be able to.

Deciding to make myself known, I step out of the shadows I was hiding in. "If you're looking for porn, babe, we can always make our own." I smirk at her.

Emily jumps out of her skin. She presses a few buttons on the computer quickly and slams the lid closed. She looks guilty as shit, like she just got caught stealing cookies from the cookie jar. The guilt quickly morphs into worry and trepidation. *Fear.*

This look, I've seen it many times, across many faces. I usually relish this look. But I never want to see this look on her. Am I pissed as fuck that she's hiding shit from me? Fuck yes, I am. But am I about to take out my frustrations on her? Fuck no.

She needs to learn that there is nothing she has to fear from me. "So, is that a yes to the home porno? Because I can have a camera set up in a few seconds. Want to play the role of my naughty secretary?" I ask as I approach the desk. She doesn't move, doesn't even blink.

Walking around the desk, I move the laptop out of the way before picking her up and sitting her in its place. I take the seat in the chair she's just vacated. I run my fingertips along the inside of her thighs, pulling the fabric of her already short dress up higher.

"You know, I don't need the camera. There is no way I'll ever forget the vision you're giving me right now, babe." I bend down and lick and nibble on her inner thigh. This started out as a way for me to ease her fear. But now, this is about me getting a taste of that delicious pussy currently staring me in the face and begging me to drink from it.

"I forgot to get my drink. I think I might just drink from here instead," I say as I move the lace panties aside, her wet, pink folds now unobstructed.

CHAPTER FIFTEEN

EMILY

*O*h my God! Did he say he's going to drink from me? Is he playing games with me here? I can't tell. I hate that I can't tell. He just caught me red-handed on his laptop, which was password protected, not that the password was hard to figure out.

I tried to search my name, to see if there was any news about me or what I had done. I got nothing, not a goddamn thing. No one is looking for me. I searched Trent's name, and again, nothing. Does that mean nobody has found his body yet? Is he still lying in a pool of his own blood on the kitchen floor?

I don't know why Josh isn't mad that I was on his computer. Why is he acting like everything is fine?

"Emmy?" His husky voice breaks me out of my internal monologue.

"Uh-uh?"

"Mind if I quench my thirst?" He smirks at me.

"Is that even a real question? If you don't, I'm sure I can find someone else who will." As soon as the words are out of my mouth, I know I've made a mistake.

Josh growls and his fingers dig into my thighs, spreading them wider than they already are. "Emily, if you ever let another man near my pussy, you'll be signing their death certificates. Because I will fucking kill them." He looks me dead in the eyes. It's not his words that tell me just how serious he is, or the fact that he said Emily and not Emmy. It's his eyes. The soul-piercing icy stare, the same gaze I imagine the devil would have.

But isn't that exactly who I've been in love with all my life? The devil currently staring back at me? I smile at him.

"I'd help you bury the bodies. Because I promise, if another man got anywhere near me, it wouldn't be because I wanted him to. Now you, on the other hand... I very much want you near me, on me, in me."

"Fuck, Emmy!" Josh grunts out, as he buries his face in the apex of my legs again. He doesn't waste any time before his tongue is slicing between my folds. My head falls back against the desk.

"Oh God, don't stop," I moan. Josh's hands go under my ass as he lifts my hips off the table, his tongue alternating between pumping in and out of my centre and circling around my clit.

My hands fist his hair, pushing his face into me,

while attempting to hold him still in just that one spot. That spot that's going to let me fly over the edge. He doesn't let me control the show. The more I pull and push on his head, the further away he moves from the spot I want him licking.

"Argh, I'm so close!" I groan. I feel him laugh, the vibrations going straight through me. He's torturing me on purpose, keeping me hanging off the edge with just enough promise of ecstasy but not delivering.

"Josh, please, I-I need." What is it that I need? I don't even know anymore.

"I'll give you everything you need and more, Emmy. All you have to do is ask," Josh says, peering up at me. I have a feeling he's talking about more than just making me come.

"I need to come, damn it," I growl. Why did he take his tongue off me?

"Your wish is my command." He smirks.

He inserts two fingers into me, while his tongue goes straight for the kill spot. I detonate. Stars, fog, the whole thing. My body quivers, and my pussy grips his fingers as my release gushes out of me.

Josh doesn't stop licking, drinking until I'm nothing but a puddle of electrified nerve endings, sprawled out on his desk. He kisses his way up my body, his lips claiming mine. Tasting myself on him turns me on way more than I ever thought it would.

Fuck, I want him. I want him so much it scares the shit out of me. This isn't healthy; I can see that. But right now, I don't care. All I can focus on is getting access to his cock. I push him back until he's sitting in his chair again.

Smiling, I slide off the desk, kneeling in front of him. It's my turn. Let's see how much he likes being kept within arm's reach of nirvana. My hands grasp for his belt. I keep eye contact with him as I undo the loops and then move onto getting his jeans undone.

Josh holds my hands still. "Emmy, you don't have to do this." His voice is strained, like although he means every word he says, he doesn't actually want to say them.

"But I want to. Do you not want me to?" I ask.

He lets go of my hands. "I want it. More than you fucking know," he grunts.

I go back to my task of freeing him from his jeans. I smile as I achieve my goal, my mouth watering at the sight of his hard cock, precum dripping from the top. My tongue glides easily along the tip, licking up what he's offering.

His taste is a little salty, musky. My hand wraps around, firmly gripping his length as I glide my arm up and down. I take turns pumping him with my hand, and running my tongue along the underside of his cock, from his balls right up to the tip, twirling around the top.

"Fuck, Emmy!" Josh growls, but other than his hips slightly pumping upwards with each stroke I make, he doesn't move. His hands grip the armrests of his chair, his knuckles white with the force.

After five minutes of teasing, I can't take it any

longer. I need him in my mouth. I slide my lips down over his length. My hand grips onto the base of him. I can't fit the whole of him in my mouth.

I close my eyes, savouring the feel of him, the taste of him. I groan around him, his thighs shaking underneath my arms. I want to make him feel good. I've had a few boyfriends, but I've never wanted to please someone as much as I want to please Josh right now. I need it. I need him to lose control because of me.

Is it a healthy feeling? Probably not. I know Josh thinks he's the one with issues here, but he doesn't know the depth of my instabilities yet. He doesn't know the things I've done over the last few years to survive.

I continue to suck and stroke his length. After a very short few minutes, Josh growls out, "Fuck, Emmy, I'm going to come." Is he really warning me? Like I'm going to suddenly pull away? I increase my efforts, sucking harder. My free hand cups his balls and rolls them around.

Josh grunts as he comes, the warm liquid filling my mouth. I swallow as quickly as I can, not wanting to waste anything he's willing to give me.

Once he's completely finished, and I've licked his length clean, Josh leans down and lifts me under my arms, bringing me up to straddle his lap. He holds me close, my head leaning on his chest as both of our hearts beat rapidly.

Josh runs his fingers through my hair, something I've noticed he does a lot. It's a nice feeling, comforting somehow. Maybe it's because I haven't felt cherished like this for a very long time.

"I know I don't deserve you. I haven't done anything good enough to have someone like you fall into my lap. But I'll be damned if I'm ever going to give you up again, Emmy."

"I don't want you to give me up, Josh. But some things are even out of your control," I tell him.

"There is nothing that is going to keep me away from you, Emmy. I don't care what I have to do. I know you don't want to tell me what you're running from. But know that I will find out, and whether you like it or not, I will fix this for you, for us." He kisses the top of my head.

I don't know what to say in response to that. I don't know how to get him to stop looking. He's going to think very differently about me if he discovers what I've done. The best thing for him would be to forget about me again. I need to figure a way out of this mess. I can't let Josh drag himself down with me.

"YOU KNOW WHAT WE NEED?" Ella asks. She's currently sitting on the daybed next to me, sipping at some concoction in a fancy glass with a little umbrella. They just keep bringing these drinks out to us.

We've been lazing by the pool all afternoon, drinking and eating ourselves into a food coma. Now Ella's all pepped up again.

"No, what do we need?" I laugh. It may be the drinks, but I like the free feeling I currently have. I'm not lost in my internal monologue, my own inner nightmare, for once. I just feel free.

"We need to go dancing. Yep, get up. We're going dancing." She jumps up and pulls at my arm.

"Dancing, I can't go dancing. Besides, look around, Ella. We're in the middle of bloody Timbuctoo. Where do you think there is to go dancing around here?" I wave my arms.

"Well, I just happen to know a little country pub about thirty minutes down the road." She smiles, proud of herself.

"I know the place you're thinking of. I went to school in this town, remember? That's not a pub we need to be at." How can I talk her out of wanting to go out? What if someone notices me? Although it appears nobody is even looking for me, which just freaks me out more. There is no way they haven't discovered what I've done.

"Come on, get up. It'll be fun. Besides, I need to go dancing. I need to let off some steam." She pouts at me.

"What about Josh?" I ask. There is no way we're both getting off this farm without him noticing. He thinks I haven't seen him lurking in the shadows every twenty minutes, watching us. But I've noticed. He stands there for at least five minutes before going back inside. Then twenty minutes later, he comes back out and watches again.

"Emily, I grew up with two very overbearing big

KYLIE KENT

brothers. I know a thing or two about sneaking out. *Trust me.* No one's going to notice we're gone until it's too late." She winks.

This could be my opportunity to get away from Josh, before I drag him down into my mess. My heart hurts at the thought of leaving him. Although I know it's for the best, it's the last thing I want to do.

"Okay, let's do it. But we need to change first. We cannot go into that pub looking like this." I point to both of our bikini-clad bodies.

"Woohoo, yes! You're already my favourite sister-in-law," Ella shrieks.

"I'm not your sister-in-law, Ella," I remind her for what seems to be the tenth time today.

"*Yet*, but you will be," she says as she takes hold of my hand and drags me through the house like she owns the place, which, I guess, she kind of does.

⌁

SITTING IN THE BOOTH, in this little old country pub, I can't help the feeling of being watched. I've been overtly looking around for the last half an hour, trying to figure out who it is that's watching me.

"Will you stop? You look like you just robbed a bank and are waiting for the cops to burst in here looking for you," Ella says from the other side of the booth.

She looks hot as hell and has not been short on drawing the attention of everyone in here. She's wearing a denim skirt and a black singlet, complemented by a pair of tan and black Ariat cowgirl boots. Her dark hair falls in two perfectly sculpted braids.

I'm not sure where the hell she got these outfits from; it's almost like she was planning this trip for longer than she admits. She put me in a little pair of denim cutoffs and a white blouse that falls off one shoulder. I'm also wearing a pair of tan and aqua Ariat boots, my hair hanging in loose curls.

When I looked in the mirror before leaving the house, the first thought I had was that I looked like me. The old me, the naïve eighteen-year-old, who left this little country town without so much as a plan.

Unlike now. Now, I do have a plan. A plan, which involves sneaking out the back door of this pub and hitchhiking out of this town. I don't care where I end up. I just know I need to get my mess away from Josh. I shouldn't have come back here. He shouldn't be dealing with my issues.

"Ella, can you promise me something?" I ask her.

"Depends on what it is," she answers while sipping at her beer. With each sip, she screws her face up. She hates it, but refused to order anything else in a pub.

"Promise me you'll look out for Josh when I'm not around anymore."

Ella puts her drink down before gripping my hand. "You're not going anywhere, Emily. I get that you think you probably need to, but please reconsider whatever it is you're planning. Josh needs you just as much as you need him. Don't do this to him, please."

"I'm not planning anything; some things are just out of our control," I lie. "I've gotta pee. Can you order me another beer please?" I ask her.

"Sure," Ella says with a sad smile. I think she knows something. But how could she possibly know what I'm planning to do?

I give her the bright, fake smile I mastered in high school and head towards the bathroom. Once I make it to the hallway, I chuck a left and head through the back kitchen area. No one even looks in my direction as I beeline for the back door. My heart hammers the whole way.

What am I actually doing? I don't want to leave. But I can't stay either. I'm doing the right thing by Josh. I have to leave so he doesn't get in trouble for me being around.

I push the heavy door open and step out into the alleyway. The door closes with a loud clanging sound of metal hitting metal. I get two steps down the alley before a hand wraps around my mouth and I'm pushed into the wall.

CHAPTER SIXTEEN

JOSH

I've been looking into finding out everything I possibly can about Trent Owens—the name Emily was looking up on my laptop. Her search didn't bring any results. So far, I've managed to discover he's a dirty fucking cop who lives in Adelaide. What the fuck is his connection to Emily?

She also searched her own name, which again, brought up no results. Just like Sam said, it's as if Emily never existed. I know that she's been abused. I can see the signs. I can still see the slight yellow bruises. If it was this Trent asshole who caused them, I at least now have a target to unleash my demons on.

Then I remember that there is someone else deserving of my wrath. Someone here on this farm who I've yet to deal with.

I make my way to the shed where that fucking stable hand is being kept on ice. The stale stench assaults me as soon as I walk through the doors. The smell of faeces and piss (as well as the stench of the fucker's fear) hangs in the air.

Pulling my shirt over my head, I hand it to one of the guys standing at the door. In return, he gives me a questioning look. "It's one of my favourites. I don't want to get blood on it." I shrug.

"What's your name?" I ask the fucker who's hanging limply from the chains.

One of his eyes is already swollen shut. He stares at me through the other, as he contemplates how to answer the simple question.

"It really doesn't matter either way, but I do prefer to know the names of stupid cunts. I'd hate to one day call my children the name of some dead fucker who should have known better."

I walk slowly over to the table, which is currently housing a lineup of knives. I pick up a big, heavy, serrated blade and weigh it around in my hands. Putting it down again, I choose a lighter one.

Just for dramatics, I pick up the whetstone and start polishing the blade, even though it's already razor sharp.

"You still haven't given me a name," I say as I stop in front of the fucker.

"Glen. The name's Glen." He shakes as he speaks.

"Glen, how long have you worked here?" I ask him.

"Three years, sir," he says proudly. I'm not sure what the fuck he's proud about.

"Three years. I'm sure within those years, you've heard of how I can sometimes be a little... *unstable*. So why the fuck would you think it's a good idea to corner my girlfriend in a fucking stable in her own home?" I scream.

The word girlfriend does not sit well with me. Emily is so much more than a girlfriend, although I'm not sure there is a word to describe what she is to me. I might settle for wife. I wonder if I can get away with a quick wedding like my brother somehow managed. He married Ella over a fucking dinner with her family. Papers signed, sealed and delivered within hours.

"I-I-I didn't know she was your girlfriend, sir."

"So that makes it all right? You didn't know she belonged to me, so you have the right to scare her and trap her in a stable?" I ask.

"No."

"That's right. Unfortunately for you, she does belong to me, which means I plan on making an example out of you. I can't exactly have people thinking they can mess with what's mine. Especially her."

I walk around him, debating what I'm going to do first. All of my pent-up anger, resentment and frustrations are about to be unleashed on this fucker.

THREE HOURS, that's how long I dragged out Glen's death, keeping him conscious enough to know what was happening and that the end was near, but not giving him the out he so desperately begged for. It was gruesome—probably some of my best work yet.

I had three men in that room run for a trash can to empty their stomachs. I'm debating whether or not I need fuckers that weak on my security detail. If they can't handle a little blood and guts, then what good are they?

Finally showered, in clean clothes and sitting back at my desk, I'm about to start digging into this Trent fucker when Paul enters the office.

"Ah, boss?" he asks pensively, stepping inside with a look I don't ever like to see on the face of my head of security.

"What happened?" I ask, getting up and walking around the desk.

"Nothing, *yet*. But Mrs. McKinley and Emily are about to head into town. They're planning on going to Hughes Pub," he says.

"Ella and Emily are going to Hughes? Follow them, but not close enough that they know. I want at least five men placed around the pub before they even enter." Picking up my wallet, phone and keys, I'm out the door.

Let's see what trouble these two find themselves in at Hughes. Why the fuck Emily would go there, I have no idea. Ella, I get; she doesn't know how rough that place can be. She also has a rebellious streak. But Emily doesn't have a rebellious bone in her body; she's the straight-A student. The kid who was literally friends with everyone and couldn't stand the thought of someone not liking her. That someone being me. She knows what Hughes Pub is like, the kind of people who choose to hang out there. Why the fuck would she want to go there?

Unless she's still got it in her head that she needs to leave... No, she can't. I won't let her destroy us before we've even had a chance to begin.

"Paul, I want your eyes on Emily the whole time. Do not let her out of your sight. Have someone at the front door. I'll be at the back door behind the pub," I demand. I'm struggling to contain my anger right now. The thought of losing her again does not sit well with me.

"Sure, boss," he says as he leaves, already talking into his earpiece.

Heading out to the garage, I jump on my black Ducati Superleggera V4, choosing speed over anything else right now. I want to be able to get to the pub before the girls arrive. I want to see them walk in. And if my suspicions are right, I want to be there at the back door when Emily walks out.

The whole way to the pub, I hope that I'm wrong. I know... hope is a bitch, but I really fucking want to be wrong about this. Can I really keep her here if she doesn't want to be here? No, I can't. I know she wants to be here; I know she thinks she's doing the right thing by wanting to leave.

If only she would tell me what the fuck has her running scared, I'd be able to fucking fix it. We'd be able to move forward. I want more than anything to help her, to give her the future she should have already had.

Pulling in behind the bar, I hide the bike next to a dumpster and wait. About fifteen minutes is all it takes for Ella and Emily to pull up in a fucking town car. How the fuck did Ella manage to get a town car all the way out here? Maybe she's a little more resourceful than I gave her credit for.

I am a little impressed, that is, until they come into full view and I see what they're both fucking wearing. Or, more accurately, what they're not wearing, which would be fucking clothes. My eyes are pinned on Emily; she's wearing little fucking denim shorts with a white shirt that doesn't even cover both shoulders. Those damn cowgirl boots she's wearing are going to look fucking good wrapped around my waist later tonight.

I have to adjust myself in my jeans; just the sight of her has my cock hard as a fucking rock. The thought of every other fucking guy in that bar getting their eyes on her is not sitting well with me.

As much as I want to barge in there and drag her ass back home, I can't. I need to know if she's planning to run or not. I need to know if I'm all in, while she's got one foot out the door. It's driving me fucking insane, more than I usually fucking am.

After twenty minutes of waiting, that little fucking

bitch, hope, makes an appearance again. I know better than to entertain her, but I do anyway, that is, until the back door slams open and shut and out walks a leggy blonde—one I know very well.

I can't believe she's doing this. She's in a fucking back alley. Anything could happen to her out here. Is she that hell-bent on leaving that she's willing to put herself in danger?

As soon as the door shuts, my hand wraps around her mouth and I'm pushing her up against the brick wall. I'm an asshole, I know, but we've also already established this. I let my emotions get the better of me, which is always the fucking case when it comes to Emily.

"Going somewhere, Emmy?" I ask into her ear.

I feel her whole body relax when she notices it's me who's got a hold of her. Where most other people would be shitting themselves, she's thanking the gods that it's me and not someone else.

She shakes her head no before biting down hard on my hand and stomping on my foot. The shock of her standing up for herself makes me loosen my grip. She doesn't miss the opportunity to slip out of my grip and turn around. When she does, I'm staring down the barrel of a Glock.

I can't help but be proud of her right now. She's taking a stand; she's showing the fighting spirit that I always knew she had. And I fucking love it.

"What on earth are you smiling at, Josh?" she asks, not moving the gun at all.

"A couple of things really. One, I'm so fucking proud of you right now—you have no idea. Two, you look hot as fuck. And three, if it's at all possible, I think I might have fallen in love with you even more in the last minute."

"That's messed up. You realise I'm the one pointing a gun at you, right? You should be hating me right now. You should want nothing to do with me. You should be moving away, not closer!" she screams.

"Emmy, there is nothing you could possibly do that would make me hate you, *ever*! I want everything to do with you, and I'm never walking away. You step back, I'm following you."

"No, Josh, you need to let me go." Her voice is quiet, her hands shaking a little.

"You're going to have to shoot me then. Because I'm not letting you fucking leave me, Emmy. Why? Tell me why? Tell me what the hell has you so determined to leave me? I know I can be a little much at times. Okay, *all the fucking time*. But I love you, Emmy. I've loved you since I was fifteen. I'd do anything for you. I want to give you the fucking world at your fingertips. Why is it not good enough?"

"You are enough, Josh. You've always been enough. I'm the one who's not okay. I messed up. I did something bad. I can't fix what I did. I can make sure that my mess doesn't get you in trouble though… and that's what I'm doing. I need to leave to protect you. Because I love you." Emmy drops the gun to her side, tears streaming down her face.

I wrap my arms around her. I don't care if she shoots me or not. I'm not fucking letting go. "You know that's the first time you've ever said I love you to me," I say, my voice hoarse. I feel tears on my own cheeks.

Emmy reaches up and wipes my face with her hands. "You are enough, Josh. Any girl would be blessed as hell to be loved by you. I'm sorry… I'm so sorry I can't give you what you need."

"All I need is you, Emmy. I don't need anything else, just you." I lean down gently, kissing her lips.

"You have me, Josh. You've always had me," she says. I can tell she still thinks she needs to leave.

"Let's go home." I'm not taking any chances on her not coming home with me. If she thinks she is staying out here on these streets, I'll be staying right here with her.

"Okay, take me home, Josh."

After calling Paul and telling him to drag Ella's ass home, I tighten my helmet on Emily's head and sit her in front of me on the bike. I don't rush home. I want time to just be with Emily without words, just us. That's what we need, time to be *just us* without any other outside forces playing against us. I know just the place we can go to do that.

CHAPTER SEVENTEEN

EMILY

"*E*mmy, babe, wake up." Josh is kissing me all over my face. I slap a hand out to stop him. When I try to roll over to avoid him, he jumps on top of me, straddling my thighs.

"Why? I just want to sleep," I complain, slowly opening my eyes.

"I have a surprise," he says excitedly.

"That's nice. I hope you enjoy it."

"The surprise is for you, Emmy. Wake up." His fingers find my waist and start circling underneath my shirt.

I'm instantly awake. My eyes spring open. My hands land on his forearms, attempting to stop his movements.

"Okay, okay, I'm awake. Stop, please. I'll wake up." I laugh as my body thrashes under his attack.

"You'll wake up?" he asks.

"Yes, I'm awake." My hands are still on his forearms. As they roam up and down, it occurs to me that they are the definition of arm porn. Strong, muscled, tattooed arms. Arms that I feel the safest in, the most cherished in.

"You have nice arms," I blurt out. Josh laughs.

"Yeah? You like my arms? What else do you like?" he asks, lifting his shirt a little and showing off his abs, his very well-defined abs.

My eyes travel from the top of his jeans up to his chest. He's fully dressed. Where is he going?

"Why do you look so nice? Are you going somewhere?"

"Thank you. And yes, I am going somewhere. With you. *We* are going somewhere. Just as soon as you get up."

"Okay, but where are we going?" I ask. "Also, you need to get off me if you want me to get up."

"I really fucking like being on top of you. But we do need to get going. I left a dress for you in the bathroom," Josh says as he stands.

My body freezes. He left a dress for me in the bathroom? This is how it starts; he's going to control me just like Trent did. Why did I think he would be any different? The only difference is it hurts so much more, because it's Josh. I've built him up so much, put him on a pedestal so high, I can't even reach it.

But when it comes down to it, they're all the same. Men just want to control me, hurt me. I'm looking at the door and calculating if I can make it there before he catches me. I can't, so my eyes search the room for anything that I can use to defend myself, or cushion the blow.

"Babe, did you hear what I said?" Josh's voice breaks through my internal hell.

I should have been listening. What's he going to do when he finds out I wasn't paying attention? I don't know what to say, so I don't say anything at all.

"What's wrong?" he asks as he walks back towards me.

"Uh, nothing. I'll get dressed. Thank you." My voice is robotic, monotone, just how Trent used to prefer me to answer.

"Something's wrong. Whatever is going through that pretty little head, forget it. You are safe here, Emmy. If you have something to say, then say it. I want you to say what's on your mind. I want to be the one you tell your secrets to, the one you share your fears with, your happy thoughts with. I want them all. I'm selfish like that." He winks before pulling my stiff body into his arms.

"I… what if I don't like the dress? Will you be mad?" I whisper.

Josh pulls his head back and tilts my chin up. I flinch away from his touch. I see his jaw clench, his eyes narrow, and he takes a deep breath. I wait for it, for his anger over my question.

When his eyes open, all I see in them is love, patience and understanding. "Emmy, if you don't like the dress, throw it out. I don't care what you wear. You wear whatever you want. I didn't pick the dress to take away your choice. Ella left it at the door this morning and said to give it to you. I just moved it to the bathroom. That's all."

I feel so stupid. Why do I always think the worst? Why do my thoughts always put Josh in the same category as Trent? He has never done anything to deserve my doubt.

Well, maybe all the shit he did in high school… But we all do stupid shit when we're young.

"I'm sorry. I don't know… I'm sorry," I tell him. I don't even know how to explain what was going through my mind.

"You have nothing to be sorry about, Emmy. Now, how about we finish getting ready so I can show you the surprise?"

"Okay."

⌣

AN HOUR LATER, we are pulling up to a private airstrip. I wait for Josh to come around and open my door; he has a thing about wanting to open my door all the time. To be honest, I like it. Stepping out, I hold down the fabric of the dress I'm wearing to make sure it doesn't blow up in the wind.

The dress Ella left was beautiful. A bright yellow

sundress. It has a corset waist with a light cotton fabric skirt that hangs loosely to the midpoint of my thighs. I put my hair up in a high ponytail, which I'm thankful for now. This wind would have played havoc on my curls.

"Why are we at an airport, Josh?" I ask him.

"I'm taking some time off. We're going to get away for a few days. Or weeks." He shrugs.

"I can't go anywhere. I don't even have a passport. Where are we going?"

"You don't need one for where we are going. And we are going to one of the family vacation homes. Don't worry, we're not leaving the country. Come on." He takes hold of my hand and starts leading me towards the runway, where there is a small jet with the McKinley Industries logo on the side of it.

"You have a jet?" I ask. Of course, the McKinleys have a jet. Is there anything they don't have?

"You know all of this is going to be yours when I can talk you into marrying me?" Josh laughs.

But I don't laugh. I try to smile at him, but it's strained. I'm not sure that I can ever get married so I decide to change the subject. It's not a discussion I can have right now.

"So how long is the trip?" I ask.

"It's a few hours. But don't worry, I've got plenty of ideas on how we can use the time wisely." He smirks.

"Oh yeah, did you pack a deck of cards or something?"

"I was thinking more along the lines of the mile

high club kind of activities. You ever joined the mile high club?" he asks.

I'm just about to tell him no, that I have not, when he interrupts me.

"Don't answer that. I was thinking today could be a day where I don't have to kill anyone."

"You wouldn't actually kill them. But, just in case you're still wondering, no, I have not ever joined the mile high club."

"Make no mistake, Emmy, I'm crazy enough to kill any fucker who has ever laid a hand on you. Whether you wanted them to or not. You and I both already know that."

What the hell do you say to that? I have nothing. Again, Josh leaves me speechless. Somehow, I do believe he is just that crazy. I remember the look he had when he was holding the knife to that guy's throat in the stable. He was more than ready to take his life. And he wouldn't lose any sleep over it.

Me? I took a life and I'm left with his ghost haunting my dreams every night... and this god-awful feeling of someone watching me constantly. I look back over my shoulder and I swear I see a figure in the distance next to a shed. My steps stop and I look again. Is this it? Has someone found me?

"Emmy, you good?" Josh asks.

"Ah, yeah, sorry. I thought I saw someone." I turn back around and continue walking. Josh glares over his shoulder in the direction I was looking, then he turns back and wraps his arm around me. He starts typing out a message as he guides me up the stairs of the plane.

I stop at the entrance of the cabin. This is not an ordinary plane. This is fancy with a capital F. I feel so out of place. When I see the two stewardesses glaring in my direction, I want nothing more than to run off the plane.

Their looks change when they see Josh step in behind me. "Mr. McKinley, welcome back. I've set up your usual spot with your drink ready for you. I'm sorry... I didn't realise you were bringing a guest. Can I get you anything else?" The blonde bombshell bats her lashes at him.

I don't like her. I'm ready to rip those eyelashes off her damn pretty face. Let's see how she bats them when she doesn't have any.

"Josh?" I turn my head to look at him. "I'm gonna need you to hold my hand right now," I tell him. I figure holding hands helps calm his fire down, so maybe it will help with mine.

Josh's eyes open in surprise. He looks from me to the stewardess. He takes hold of my hand, pulling me into him. His lips slam down on mine and he claims me in front of both stewardesses. I do nothing to stop him; instead, my tongue hungrily meets his.

When he finally pulls away, he smiles down at me before turning to the stewardess. "Crystal is it?" he asks the blonde one.

"Yes, sir." She beams at him.

"You're fired. Get the fuck off my plane," he growls as he walks past her, dragging me behind him.

"But-but… I've worked for your family for years. You can't just fire me," she stammers out.

Josh stops walking and steps in front of me. "You see that name embroidered onto the seats? That's my name. I very much can fire you and I just did. Don't make me repeat myself."

"Are you crazy?" she yells at him. Something in me snaps. I've always hated when people call Josh crazy. He's not crazy, just different. Okay, maybe a little crazy, but he's my kind of crazy. No one else is going to get away with calling him names.

I step in front of Josh. He lets me move him aside, allowing me to get in front of him. There's a drink on one of the side tables. I don't know what's in it or whose it is, but right now I don't care. I pick it up and throw the liquid at the stupid bitch.

"He's not crazy. But if you call him any more names, you're about to see just how *crazy* I am," I threaten over her shrieks.

"You stupid bitch!" she screams and starts charging towards me. Before I can even blink, I'm pushed behind a big body. When I finally look around the wide shoulders obstructing my view, I see that Josh has the woman up against the wall of the plane. His hand is wrapped around her throat.

Shit, this escalated way too much. Josh's body is vibrating as he holds her in place but I am blocked by the figure in front of me. I can't get to him.

"Do you want to know what happened to the last person who threatened her?" He tilts his head behind him, in my direction. The woman doesn't answer, but he continues.

"I took my time. It wasn't quick. Three hours, he held out for three hours before I finally let him die. Do you know how it feels to have your skin removed from your body, bit by bit? To watch pigs eat the fingers and toes that have been cut off? All the while, knowing the rest of your body will end up in the pigpen too?"

The girl goes white. Surely, he didn't... did he? Even though I know he's probably telling the truth, I can't bring myself to look at him any differently. I saw him shoot someone right in front of me, yet I never thought of it again. He does that to me, the Josh fog. Whenever I'm with him, it's like the rest of the world doesn't exist. It's just us.

Right now, I need that. I need it to be just me and him again. "Josh, I-I need..." I don't even know what I need. What do I say to get him to let her go? I try to step around the hulking man who's blocking my way, but he doesn't let me.

"If you don't move out of my way, I'm going to shove that gun—the one I can clearly see under your jacket—so far up your ass you'll be shitting bullets for weeks." I fold my arms over my chest and wait for the man to move.

The whole plane goes silent, all bar Josh, who is currently laughing under his breath. What the hell is so funny?

I look up at the guy in front of me; he doesn't look impressed. Oh shit, I then realise what I just said. Where the hell did that even come from? I take a step back, my throat dry.

I hear Josh yell, "Fuck!" but my eyes don't leave the hulking guy. Although he hasn't moved, my feet are still stepping away from him, that is, until my back hits a chair and I can't move any further.

CHAPTER EIGHTEEN

JOSH

Seeing Emily stick up for me, wanting to defend me, is the biggest fucking turn on ever. My cock is painfully hard right now. Hearing her threaten Paul for not letting her past him, that made my day.

My girl is starting to come out of her shell, starting to say what's really on her mind. And I fucking love it. What I don't love is the look of terror that immediately came over her face after she told him she'd shove his gun so far up his ass he'd be shitting bullets.

Not even I could have come up with that line. It's not one I'll be forgetting in a hurry. Paul might not be impressed, but I'm proud as punch with her.

"Deal with *that*. Make sure she leaves quietly," I tell Paul, motioning to the stewardess who just escaped my wrath. I have more important things on my mind now; for one, my brain is counting the minutes until we are in the air and I can finally get to bury my cock into Emily.

I can't fucking stand the look of fear on her face, and the fact that I know where that fear has come from. At least I suspect where it's come from anyway. She's afraid of repercussions for speaking out, for threatening a guy on my payroll. I don't give a shit who she wants to threaten. I'll keep reassuring her that she's safe, for as long as it takes to sink in. She never has to sensor herself around me. If anyone else doesn't like what she has to say, they can find the fucking door, because she is the queen of this castle. She just doesn't know it yet.

Walking up to her and caging her against the seat she's backed herself into, I lean down and whisper in her ear, "Emmy, you are safe here. Don't ever be afraid of anyone when I'm around. I'll never let anyone hurt you. You know that, right?"

"I'm sorry. I shouldn't have said that," she apologises.

"Yes, you should have. You should always say what's on your mind. And never be sorry for it, babe. I fucking love your mouth, every word that comes out of it. Not to mention, how it feels wrapped around my cock. Fuck!" I have to adjust my cock in my jeans. Emily looks down at my hand then back at me with wide eyes.

"I'm always hard when I'm around you, but I almost

came in my fucking jeans when you wanted to defend me. You don't need to by the way. I don't care what people say about me. But fuck, I love that you do." I kiss along the side of her neck and up to her ear, before sucking the lobe into my mouth.

Emily's arms go around my neck, and she pulls me in closer. "I don't like when people call you crazy. I never have. It makes me so angry I want to rip out their tongues and show them what crazy really looks like," she says.

I laugh. I could not imagine Emily actually doing any of that. She's always been sweet little Emmy, who is friends with everyone. The people pleaser, who always has a smile on her face, or at least she used to.

That smile was always fake—I could tell. Even when we were kids, I could see the pain and loneliness disguised behind her smiles. I love the real Emmy, the one she lets me see. I could live without watching her experience those fucking nightmares and the constant fear, but it's only been a few days and we are making progress. I don't care if it takes the rest of my life. I will get her to be the strong, confident woman I know she can be.

"Remember that time in year eleven when Jessica projectile vomited all over John in science?" she asks.

"Ah, yeah. Why?"

"Well, I overheard her in the bathroom that morning, telling Cassie how you had asked her out, but she turned you down because you were too psycho for her." Emily smiles at me, one of her bright, real smiles.

"I might have put something in her iced coffee at recess."

"You made her sick? Because you thought I asked her out?" I ask, confused.

"No, well, maybe. Mostly because she was calling you names. And a little bit because I was jealous and angry that you'd ask her out and not me." She pouts.

"Babe, I never asked her out. There was only ever one girl I wanted in high school."

"Who?" Emily pulls away from me and folds her arms over her chest.

"You, of course. I never dated or hooked up with anyone before you, Emmy," I confess. That night was not just *her* first time.

"Really, I was your first too? You were so good at it I assumed you'd done it before."

"Well, it's not exactly a hardship to love you, Emmy. Come sit, we need to get ready for takeoff."

I lead her over to one of the four sets of chairs in this cabin. As soon as we are in the air, I plan on taking her into the bedroom and not coming out until landing time. Leaning across the seat, I buckle her seat belt for her.

"Thank you?" Emily questions.

"Trust me, it's my pleasure." I have to readjust my cock yet again; he's fucking raging to get out and into his home between Emily's thighs.

"You okay over there?" Emily raises her eyebrows at me.

"No, not at all," I grunt out.

"Sir, ma'am, can I get you all anything before we take off." The second stewardess, who has just been standing in the background the whole time, timidly approaches us.

"No, I'm good. Thank you. Emily, do you need anything?" I ask her. She's chewing on her bottom lip, contemplating if she can request something or not.

"Babe, whatever you want, I'll make sure you get it. What do you need?" I prompt.

"Uh, do you have a blanket at all?" Emily asks the stewardess.

"Yes, absolutely. I'll go get you one now." The stewardess, who's name I really should learn, walks away like her heels are on fire.

"You cold? Want me to get you a jacket?" I ask her. Why didn't I think to bring a jacket for her?

Emily shakes her head shyly. "I'm okay. A blanket is fine."

"Here you go, ma'am. Please let me know if you need anything else. We're about to take off any minute." The stewardess walks away.

Emily kicks off her heels and folds her feet underneath her on the armchair. She places the blanket over her lap before stretching it out and spreading some of it over my thighs.

"Emmy, you don't need to share the blanket with me. I'm not cold. You keep it." I go to pull it off me, intending to wrap the whole thing around her legs, when she stops my movements.

"You need the blanket, Josh, trust me," she says sternly.

"Yes, ma'am." I laugh and keep the blanket on my lap. I'm not about to contradict her when she's being so forceful and insistent.

The plane starts its trip down the runway, with it, Emmy's hand lands on my knee, slowly creeping its way up my thigh. I don't stop her explorations. It's fucking hard (pun intended) not to grab her hand and place it directly over my cock.

Just as the plane takes off from the runway, Emily's fingers are undoing my belt, then my button, slowly unzipping my fly. The moment her tiny hand wraps around my cock, I let out the moan I've been fighting off.

"Argh, fuck!" My hips lift off the seat with her first stroke. Her thumb swirls around the tip, collecting the precum that's dripping freely. She lets go of my cock, and I'm just about to take her hand and force it back on there, when I watch her bring her thumb up to her mouth and suck it in.

Her eyes close with the gesture. "Jesus, are you purposely trying to kill me, woman? Because it's fucking working," I growl.

Her eyes now open, she releases her thumb with a plop sound. "No, I just wanted to get a taste of my new favourite flavour." She's quick to wrap her hand back around my cock. This time, she gets right to pumping me up and down.

Her grip firm, her strokes are a perfect mixture of

fast and slow. I need to get inside her pussy now. If I can't get my cock in there, my fingers are going to have to be buried in her. The moment my hand slides under the blanket and up her thigh, she moves it away.

"Fuck, babe, I need to feel that sweet fucking pussy of yours," I grunt out.

"You want to feel how wet I am for you right now? Feel the juices dripping from me?" she asks.

Her words shock me, yet turn me on more *if that's possible*. "Fuck yes I do!" I pant as she increases the speed of her strokes.

"Mmm, you're going to have to wait. I'm busy right now, and I don't want to be distracted."

"Please, I need it," I beg. When she just shakes her head no, I have to ask, "At least tell me, are you dripping wet for me, Emmy. Is your pussy craving to be filled by my cock right now?"

"Yes." Her voice is husky, her cheeks flushed red as her body leans into me more. With that one word, I come hard all over her hand and my jeans.

"Fuck, Emmy, God!" I moan loudly, not giving a fuck who hears me. She might have wanted the blanket for privacy, but I don't give a shit who knows what we're up to back here.

"Shh, everyone is going to hear you," she whispers harshly.

"Let them. I want everyone to know that you're mine!" I tell her right as the seat belt sign goes off.

Thank God, finally. I rip both of our seat belts off, scoop Emily up and carry her into the bedroom.

"Wait, what? Oh my God, your plane has a bedroom?" She squeals as I throw us both down on the bed. Me, on my back. Her, on top of me.

"We can discuss the floor plan of the plane later, Em. My cock needs to be buried inside you now," I growl as I unzip the zipper at the back of her dress.

"Oh, but you just, wow, okay," she says. I pull the dress over her head, her breasts bouncing free right in front of my face. She's left in only a pair of the littlest white lace panties.

"I hope you're not too attached to these," I say as my fingers trace the top of them.

"Why?" she asks.

Giving her my best smirk, I don't bother to answer her. Grabbing the material in both hands, I rip the lace in two. Then, lifting her hips, I position my cock at her entrance. Emmy's eyes go wide as I slowly sink her down onto me.

"Ah, fuck, this is fucking heaven," I moan, her tight, wet pussy gripping my cock like a damn glove. Once she's fully seated, she looks at me with shock. "This… is…" She cuts her sentence short. She seems unsure.

"This is…?" I push her to continue, pumping my hips up. She squeaks (yes, *squeaks*).

"Oh, God. That's good. It feels different," she says as she slowly wiggles around. I'm restraining myself from coming again already.

"Different? How? Good or bad?"

"Oh, it's good. I just don't know. I don't think I'm good at this. I've never…"

"You've never what?" I ask her confused. Then it hits me, she's never been on top before.

"You've never been on top before?" I smile as I repeat the sudden revelation.

"No, I wasn't allow..." Again, she stops mid-sentence. But I got enough to know what she was going to say. I lay my hands under my head. As much as I want to take control and fuck her into the next galaxy, I want to give her something she desperately needs. I want to give her control, choice with her body and over what she's doing.

"This is your show, Emmy. You are in control. And trust me, there is no way you could do it wrong. Just having you sitting on my cock right now is everything right in the world. You do whatever you want to me. Nothing's off limits." I smirk and wait her out.

It takes only a minute before she smiles. "Anything I want?" she repeats.

"Anything," I confirm.

"Okay, but will you tell me if you don't like it?" she asks shyly.

"Sure," I lie. If she discovers something that she *does* like, I'll learn to love it if I have to. I'm not going to take this away from her. She's a goddamn fucking queen, and it's about time she realises it.

CHAPTER NINETEEN

EMILY

*O*h my God, I can't believe how good this feels. I've never been on top before. I didn't realise it would be so different. The kind of control I have right now is intoxicating. Josh is doing this for me. Handing the reins over, no matter how much I can see that he wants to take me. He's letting me explore, letting me feel like I have a say in how this goes.

My hands slide up under his shirt. Why the hell is he still dressed? This needs to change. Pulling at the fabric, I tell him, "Lose the shirt, *now!*" My hands tug it up. He obliges.

"If I must." He sits up slightly to pull the shirt over his head. His movements cause his cock to hit all different heights inside me. "Mmm, God." I grind my pelvis down on him harder, little sparks of pleasure going right through me.

My fingertips trail up his abs to his shoulder and I push him back down. I can't believe I'm doing this. I've dreamt about having my way with this body, and now I actually get to.

I run my hands over his shoulders, down his arms and back up again. Leaning over, I lick around one of his nipples, lightly biting down on it.

"Fuck, Emmy, goddamn," he grunts out.

I pop my head up and smile. "You said anything!" I shrug my shoulders before ducking my head back down. I trail my tongue over the lines and swirls that mark his chest. When I reach the spot just over his heart—the spot with my name on it—I kiss it three times. One time for our past, one for the present, and one for the future I wish we could have.

Reaching his other nipple, I suck it into my mouth, biting down a little harder than the first time. I feel his cock twitch inside me so I do it again and again, as I start to move my hips up and down.

Sitting up straight, I pull his hands out from under his head. I need him touching me. I love seeing his tanned, tattooed skin against mine. I place his hands on my breasts. I don't have to guide him on what else to do. He rolls my nipples between his fingers, twisting slightly. My back arches as I continue to glide up and down on his cock.

I'm so close to coming, goosebumps erupting on my

body as the cold air hits the tiny beads of sweat. I feel like a thousand bolts of electricity are circulating through me, and each time I bottom out on him, a flame is igniting higher and higher.

It's there. It's so close I can see it—*that release*. I just can't seem to reach it. I need something else, but I don't know what. "Josh, I need... something," I pant as I continue to chase my orgasm.

Josh sits up and repositions us with his back against the bed. His hand comes up to my throat and he squeezes lightly. It's wrong, so wrong, to let him do that. It's even more wrong that I fucking enjoy it. The moment his hand wraps around my throat, my pussy gushes liquid. I can feel it all down my thighs.

The next thing I know, my body is tightening up and my muscles spasm as I come undone. I think I'm screaming. I'm not really sure if it's in my head, or if I'm actually making those noises. I don't really care either way.

My pussy convulses around his cock, like it can't get enough of him. I feel his cock get even bigger as it jerks inside me, painting my walls with his seed. As I come down from my high, I finally have enough brain cells working to notice that we have been having a lot of sex without protection. I'm trying to recall when I'm due for my birth control shot.

I collapse onto Josh's chest. His hands stroke my hair, my mind reeling at trying to remember that bloody date. I can't for the life of me remember. I should know this. The one time I stuffed up and forgot to get it, Trent made sure I learnt a lesson I'd never forget.

"I can hear you thinking. What's wrong? Did I hurt you?" Josh picks my head up, our eyes connecting. I shake my head no.

"No, I just… I can't remember," I tell him.

"Can't remember what?"

"When I last had my birth control shot," I say quietly. I wait for him to explode, for him to throw me off in disgust. He does none of that.

"That's all you're worried about?" He leans in and kisses me, ending the gesture way too soon. "Emmy, you know if you fall pregnant, we will be okay. You'd make a fucking great mother."

"You're not worried? Josh, we can't have a baby. *I* can't have a baby. I'm flat out looking after myself. How am I supposed to look after a baby?" I ask him.

"You have me. I love you. I'd never abandon you, Emmy. You wouldn't be alone."

"Do you even want kids, Josh?" There's something about the way he's phrasing his words that doesn't sit well. He's not talking about a child; he's talking about me. He'd look after *me*. He wouldn't leave *me*. But what about the hypothetical child who would be his as well?

"I want you, Emmy. It's not that I don't want kids. Because I want everything with you. But, let's be honest, I'm not normal. What if I don't love it, the baby? That's a very real possibility. There is one person

I've met in my whole life, Emily, who I can honestly say I love, and I'm looking at her."

I think about what he's saying. He really has no idea just how great he would be as a father. If I ever do get to have a child (which, let's face it, *that* is not in my future), I wouldn't want it to be with anyone other than him.

"Josh, you are more capable of love than you give yourself credit for. You do love other people. There's your brother, your mum. Ella. It's not just me." I don't know how to get him to see how much he does love other people too.

"No, I might care about them a little. But it's not love, Emily. What I feel for you is different; it's more intense. I've never had that with anyone else."

"It's meant to be different. But that doesn't mean you don't love them. I loved my parents too, but not the same way I love you. With you, it's like you consume me, like every fibre of my being comes to life when I'm around you. I feel like I can do anything, be anything, with you. With my parents, I was heart-broken when each of them died. But the thought of something happening to you, I wouldn't survive that kind of loss. There wasn't a day that went by over the last four years that I didn't want to call you. That I wasn't thinking about you. Thoughts of you got me through some of my darkest moments."

I'm not sure I will ever be able to tell him all the details of what I've done, but he does deserve to know that he is loved, unconditionally, by me. That no one will ever measure up to him.

"Emmy, what happened to your mum?" he asks. Shit, how do I answer that? How do I tell him that I'm the reason my mum is dead?

"Emmy? You can tell me anything. There isn't a damn thing you can't tell me. What happened to her?" he presses on. I can't stop the tears from falling down my cheeks. Josh is patient. He swipes the wetness away and waits for me to speak.

"It-It was my fault. I should have known better. I shouldn't have…"

"Babe, it's okay, breathe. Try again. What was your fault?"

"My mum, he-he killed her because I tried to leave. I left… I did leave. But he found me, and the next day, he showed me… he showed me photos and a death certificate. It was my fault. If I didn't try to leave, my mum would still be here." I'm sobbing by the time I get it out. I've never said the words out loud. Oh God, I can't believe I just told Josh that. What is he going to think of me now? He's going to know that I'm the reason my mum is dead.

Josh squeezes my body tight against his; he holds my head on his chest. "I'm going to fucking rip him apart when I get my hands on that fucker," Josh growls.

He won't ever get the chance. I'm shaking. I try to snuggle in more, but I can't seem to get close enough. Maybe if I hold on tighter, he won't be able to walk away from me.

"Emmy, look at me," Josh says after a few minutes. I lift my head, expecting to see disgust on his face. Josh has a single tear trailing down his cheek. He's crying? Why?

"You didn't kill your mother, Emmy. What that bastard did to you was not your fault. And I want to know every little fucking thing he ever did. So that way, when I find the prick, he will know just what it feels like." Josh's voice is quiet, contradicting his harsh words.

I shake my head no. There is no way I can tell him everything. I can't...

"Emmy, your mum isn't dead. She's still in the same house you guys lived in when you left."

"What? No. I saw the pictures, Josh. I saw the death certificate. I went to her funeral!" I yell at him. Why is he being cruel? Is this it? Where it starts, the nastiness, the cruelty?

"Emily, stop. I'm telling you the truth. I've had someone do a little digging on you. That's how I found out there was a death certificate for you. I've seen your mother's too, but I've also seen photos of her around town. In her house. She isn't dead, Emily."

"No! You need to stop looking, Josh. You need to stop. You need to stop," I repeat the words over and over. I try to get off the bed. He doesn't let go of me.

"There will never be a day where I stop, Emily. You don't get it. I can't just let it go. I can't let that asshole breathe after what he's done to you. And I'm only guessing at what you've been through. When you're ready, you will tell me. Until then, I'm never going to stop loving you."

"Josh, she's really alive? Do you... do you have the photos?" I ask him. I need to see her, before I let myself hope.

CHAPTER TWENTY

JOSH

"*E*mmy, wake up. We're here." I kiss her forehead and run my fingers through her hair. I've just pulled up to one of the family farming properties in Western Australia. It took a five-hour plane trip and a three-hour drive to get out here. But this is the perfect spot to be alone with Emmy. No one comes to this cabin; the staff who work the farm live in housing on the other side of the property.

There is nothing to see but red dirt and dust. But I fucking love it out here. No fuckers to piss me off or get on my nerves. No need to attempt at being social, even though all I want to do is rip everyone's head off every other minute. This is the one place I've been able to just be me, without judgement.

I doubt anyone other than the staff here even knows

this cabin exists. I built it three years ago, when I needed an escape from the world. I spent six weeks out here before I went back home and faced my father's rage. People think I'm psychotic and cruel, but I've got nothing on what that man could do. At a minimum, *I* have some limits. Or, at least, I like to think I do.

Emily's not budging. I get out of the car and jog around to her door. Reaching in, I get a whiff of that scent I want to surround every room of every house I own in. Emily, she's fucking mind-alteringly intoxicating, like I'm on a constant high when she's near me.

She stirs in my arms but doesn't wake up. She exhausted herself on the plane. Her breakdown tore me in half, just seeing her fall apart like that, hearing the small snippets she told me about what that fucker Trent did to her. I bury my head into her neck and breathe in. I need to calm the inferno that's blazing inside me.

Emily deserves this getaway; she deserves some happy memories—ones filled with being loved and worshiped like the fucking goddess she is. I don't care what it takes. I will give her as many of those moments as I can.

"Mmm, where are we?" she asks as I'm walking up the steps.

"This is one of the family farms; it's secluded. There's no one out here except you and me, Em. This is what I call fucking paradise."

"Okay, I'd like to be thoughtful and tell you that you

can put me down. I won't though. I like being in your arms."

"Well, it's a good thing I like you being in my arms too."

Opening the door, I carry her through to the living room. Emily spots the windows at the back of the cabin.

"Oh my God! Josh, put me down. Put me down!" she shrieks.

"But you just said I could keep you here in my arms, Emmy."

"Yeah, but that was before I saw this. Put me down." She jumps out of my arms and practically runs over to the windows.

"Josh, it's so beautiful. I can't believe it. Look at them." She's pointing at the mob of brumbies in the fields. It's a sight, that's for sure.

"I knew your family had horses, but this is something else. Isn't it spectacular?"

"Yeah, it is. These aren't ours though, babe. These are brumbies; they're wild."

"I don't care. I love them. I could sit here for hours watching them."

"How about I cook us up something to eat. You can go sit out on the patio and watch them while you wait." I wrap my arms around her, trailing kisses up the side of her neck.

"Mmm, I can cook dinner. You've been driving for hours; you should sit down and relax."

"Emmy, go and sit outside. I'll bring you out a glass of wine. I want to cook for you. Let me cook for you."

"Okay, but I can help if you want."

"What I want is for you to go and sit down and watch the brumbies."

I wait until I see her settle into a lounge chair on the patio, before I head into the kitchen and find something to eat. I had some of the staff head up here today and stock up for us.

Deciding on omelettes, because I don't want to be away from Emmy for too long, I get all the ingredients out. I pour her a glass of red wine and put some grapes, cheese and crackers on a platter. Taking it out, I set the platter on the table next to her and hand her the wine.

"It's a little chilly out here. Do you want a blanket?" I ask her.

"Thank you. I'm not cold. I love it out here."

"Okay, I'm making omelettes. You do still eat eggs, right?"

"How did you know I ever ate eggs?" She smirks.

"I used to watch you eat in the school cafeteria. I'd watch as you'd suck on your spoon or fork and imagine that it was my cock you were wrapping your lips around." I shrug. I leave her with her mouth hanging open as I go back inside.

"I DON'T THINK I could eat another bite. Where on earth did you learn to cook like this?" Emmy says around the last forkful of food from her plate.

"I took classes. I find keeping busy helps."

"Helps with what?"

"The noise in my mind." I debate over how much to actually tell her. She knows I'm different, unhinged. But she doesn't know the extent of it. She doesn't really know how my mind works. I'm afraid if she did, she'd be running for the hills, not that I'd let her get far before I brought her back.

"Well, what else do you do to keep busy?"

I guess she's skipping the whole noise in my mind thing. She's the only person I've met that doesn't look at me like I'm crazy, or like they're scared I'm going to rip their hearts out.

"I ride?" I shrug.

"What, like horses? Bikes?"

"Horses, dirt bikes, road bikes, *you*." I smirk at her and watch the blush creep up her neck and face.

"We should go riding together someday. I haven't ridden for years."

"Well, you can ride me any day, babe. But I'm sure I can rustle up a couple of Quarterbacks for us tomorrow if you want."

"Really? Yes!"

"I'd like to think your excitement is about the riding me option. But I'm pretty sure it's more for the horses."

Emily laughs, and I fucking love it. "Well, can I pick both options?"

223

"Emmy, you can have whatever you want. All you have to do is ask."

"Did you become a genie? What do I have to rub to get my three wishes?"

"I've got something you can rub." I raise my eyebrows at her. "You don't have to do anything, Em, and your wishes are boundless—*there is no limit to what I would do for you, give you.*"

"Mmm, okay. So how does this work? I just ask for something and you make it appear?" She laughs like it's a big joke.

"Sure, try it. What's something you've always wanted but never thought you could have?"

Emily thinks about it for a minute, then looks me in the eye as she says, "You."

"Well, that's an easy one, because you've always had me. You just didn't know it. What else?"

"Um, well, I've always wanted the *Beauty and the Beast* library. When I was a little girl, I used to pretend that I was Belle and I could go and save my daddy from the bad guys he was fighting. Then he died anyway. I very quickly learnt that fairy tales don't exist."

"I'm not too sure they don't exist, Emmy. Looks to me like you found your beast, because you sure as fuck are my beauty."

"Yeah, but you're not a beast. You're the nicest person I've ever met."

Okay, now it's my turn to laugh. Shit, how the fuck am I the nicest person she's met? "I'm pretty sure literally every other fucking person would lock you up in a nut house for that sentence."

"Okay, so you're an absolute asshole, a jerk, to everyone else. But to me, you're not—well, not anymore. And that's what matters to me."

"Wait, what do you mean *not anymore*? When have I been an asshole to you?"

"We don't have enough time to rehash high school. But for one, June, year ten, science class. You made sure we were lab partners for that assignment. But then you disappeared, and I had to do the whole thing on my own."

"Nope, I wasn't an asshole. I was protecting you from having to be partnered with all the other dumb fucks in that class. Besides, that class was seventy percent males; you would have ended up being partnered with someone else. You would have ended up studying with that person after school. They would have tried to hit on you. I saved you from that whole ordeal. Really, I'm like your regular knight in shining armour."

"I'm not sure what worries me more: the fact that you truly believe your own words, or the fact that I don't actually care about all the shit from high school."

"You didn't really have that bad of a time in school, did you? I really did try to make sure everyone was nice to you." I will go back and hunt the fucking idiots down if they didn't treat her well.

"Everyone was too scared not to be nice to me, Josh. I had lots of friends, but they were only my friends because they didn't want to be on your bad side. Not to mention, those girls who thought you would notice them more if they hung out with me."

"Like I would notice anyone other than you, Em. I'm sorry if I made your final years of school horrible. I really am. I was young and stupid."

"You didn't. You know, you're the first boy I ever crushed on. I tried so bloody hard to get your attention that first year. But nothing seemed to work. Then I gave up, thinking that you were just out to make my life hell. Until that party where you told me you loved me. That was one of the best nights of my life."

"You were supposed to be asleep. I can't believe you heard that whole conversation and didn't say anything. There was more said than just the fact that I love you."

"Oh, you mean like the part where you said you wanted to kidnap me and run away somewhere? Or that part where you said that I gave you hope, that you could see a better future when you looked at me?"

"Look around you, Emmy. I essentially have kidnapped you and ran away." I laugh, waving my arms around.

"Yeah, but I came willingly. You know, I would have followed you anywhere, even back then."

"I know, which is exactly why I stayed away from you. I would have only ruined you. I probably still will ruin you."

Emily looks at me, her eyes sad. "You can't ruin me, Josh. I'm already ruined and there's not enough duct tape in the world to fix me."

I get up and squat down in front of her chair. Taking her hands in both of mine, I look her directly in her eyes. "There is absolutely nothing wrong with you, Emily. You are perfect, beautiful inside and out. Anyone that tells you otherwise can go and fuck off."

"Can I use one of those magic wishes of yours?" she asks.

"Your wish is my command." I wink.

"I wish that you would pick me up right now, kiss me like it's the last time you're ever going to get to kiss me, and take me to bed."

That's a wish I can deliver on. Picking her up, I carry her into the bedroom. I lay her down, fall on top of her and do exactly what she just wished for. Then I kiss her like it's the last time we will ever kiss.

CHAPTER TWENTY-ONE

EMILY

"*D*id you really think I'd let you get away that easily? Huh, that you could outsmart me?" he yells, picking up a vase and throwing it across the room.

"N-no, Trent, I'm sorry. I'm sorry. I wasn't thinking." I'm not sorry that I left; what I'm sorry for is that I didn't get far enough away before he found me.

"You weren't thinking. That's your damn problem, Emily. You're never fucking thinking. You keep making me punish you over and over again. Do you think I enjoy fucking punishing you?"

I know he does; the sick fuck gets off on it. "No, you don't need to punish me. I won't do it again. I promise."

"You're damn straight you won't fucking try it again. I'll make sure this is a lesson you'll never forget."

"Noooo!" I scream as I bring my hands up to cover my

face. I know that was a mistake as soon as I hear the snap of my arm.

"Emmy, wake up. Wake the fuck up!" Josh's voice is yelling at me.

My eyes snap open as I come face to face with Josh. He doesn't look so good. His jaw is clenched tight, and there's a dark storm brewing in his eyes. What happened? Why is he looking at me like that?

"Josh, what's wrong?" I ask.

"Nothing's wrong. Are you okay?"

He's lying. I can tell something is bothering him. I can tell he's on the verge of losing the plot. I'm not scared though. His hands are gripped firmly around my forearms. I wince at how tight his hold is, wriggling my arms a little. He immediately lets go and curses under his breath.

I nod my head. "I'm fine. What's wrong?" I ask again.

He doesn't say anything. Instead, he leans in and claims my mouth, his tongue circling around mine. I get lost in his kiss, in the passion, the love he puts into one simple gesture. My arms wrap around his neck, pulling him closer. No matter how close he is, it's never enough.

He pulls back, breaking my moment of bliss. "We have to leave this bubble and go home again."

"But I love our bubble. This has been the best week of my entire life. Why does it have to end?"

"I love our bubble too. Emmy, you are my bubble. It doesn't matter where we are, or who is around us—this bubble is ours to keep." Josh brings my hand up to his lips, kissing my palm before placing it over his heart. "I won't let anything destroy our bubble, Emmy."

"You can't stop the inevitable, Josh. Nothing this good lasts forever. Someone once told me that hope was a bitch best left alone."

"Well, that person was a fucking idiot, obviously." He rolls his eyes.

"Can we go riding before we leave?"

"Sure, babe. Hop up and get ready. I'll go out and saddle up the horses." He leans down and kisses my forehead before he leaves the room.

Stretching my aching muscles out before I even attempt to get out of bed, I welcome this kind of soreness. It's the result of the activities from the last week. It's been a week packed full of horse riding, hiking, and Josh. *So much Josh.* I shouldn't be enjoying intimacy after what Trent put me through for years, or at least I think I shouldn't... I've been so blissfully happy this last week here with Josh, I can almost trick my mind into believing the last few years were just a nightmare.

With Josh, everything is different. Every time we're intimate, it feels like the first time, new and exciting. He makes sure I'm always enjoying it. I've never had to fake an orgasm with him. Instead, I'm spent, fighting them off while trying not to combust every damn time he so much as touches me.

I MIGHT HAVE SPENT way too long in the shower under the hot water. When I walk out to the living room, the smell of bacon fills the air. Josh has insisted on cooking every meal since we arrived. He at least lets me help clean up afterwards. Who knew washing dishes could be so much fun?

I find Josh in the kitchen, just as he's placing a full plate on the bench. "Thought I'd have to come drag you out of the shower."

"Sorry, I lost track of time. This smells delicious." I sit down at the bench in front of a plate full of bacon, sausages, scrambled eggs and hash browns. He must have had it cooked for a while; he's already cleaned up. The kitchen is pristine. I know Josh calls this a cabin, but it's no regular cabin.

This kitchen is something out of an interior decorating magazine. Pristine white marble benchtops, dark-stained wooden cabinets. The sink is a huge, square, farm-style basin. I love it. It's got such a homey feel to it. I could almost picture raising kids here, having a little soccer team full of tiny Joshes. If only that dream was a possibility...

"Don't be sorry. *I'm* sorry I wasn't smart enough to join you in there." Josh winks.

"It would have been a lot more pleasurable if you had, but then I wouldn't have all of this in front of me right now." I shove a forkful of the fluffiest eggs into my mouth. "Mmm, damn, these are good."

"Fuck, Em, my cock just went from half to a

hundred, watching you eat eggs. It's like high school all over again."

"Except now you're not too chicken shit to talk to me." I smirk.

"Well, there's that." Josh laughs.

Over the past week, I've come out of my shell a lot. I still second guess myself (and the things I say) most times. But Josh has really put a magic spell over me, allowing me to be more myself than I've been in years. I can joke around with him and not get backhanded for talking back. I can ask him for something and he somehow makes it appear.

"Eat up. The horses are ready and there's a spot I want to show you." He points at my plate as he sits down next to me.

"You mean there's still places we haven't been to yet?" We've spent hours out on the horses every day we've been here. I love it. It's so freeing, being in the bush on horseback and riding through all the trails.

Josh laughs. "Babe, this property is over three hundred hectares. We've barely scratched the surface."

I shovel the food into my mouth, eager to get back out on the horses. It takes me no longer than ten minutes to finish the whole plate. "Okay, I'm ready."

"Well, don't let me keep you. Let's go," Josh says, grabbing my hand and leading me outside.

"Hi, Cherry girl," I coo at the horse I've come to think of as my new best friend. Josh approaches me with the helmet he insists I wear, even though he doesn't bother wearing one himself.

"Thank you." I'm not going to admit it any time soon, but I secretly love his protectiveness over me.

"Jump up." He waits for me to be settled on Cherry before getting on Herbert. Herbert's a big, brown, grumpy Quarterback who's perfectly matched to Josh.

"Lead the way." I smile as innocently as I can. I love riding behind him. I get to watch that perfect ass of his bounce around.

"Try not to get too distracted." Josh smirks as he leads us out into the fields.

It takes an hour for Josh to pull up to a stop. He jumps down from Herbert. I follow his lead and dismount from Cherry. However, I may have been a little too distracted by that ass of his in those tight denim jeans, because I somehow misstep and end up falling. I let out a little squeal as I land on my side, my left hip and arm hitting the ground.

Within seconds, Josh is by my side, panic clear all over his face.

"Fuck, Emmy, are you okay? No, of course you're not okay. Fuck. Stay still. Don't move. Where does it hurt?"

I can't help but laugh. I go to get up but he stops me. "Emily, do not move. What if somethings broken? You just fell off a fucking horse. Stay still." He pulls at his hair and looks around the bush we're currently isolated in, like somehow someone's going to pop out and help him.

"Joshua, stop it. I'm fine. I didn't fall off the horse. I just misstepped. That's all. It's just a scrape, see?" I hold my arm out for him to have a look—it really *is* just a scrape. I'm not sure if I should tell him my hip hurts like hell though. I can already feel the bruise forming.

"You're not fine. You're bleeding, Emmy. Shit, what do I do? Should I call the helipad? Fuck, there's a doctor on the farm. I'll get him to meet us at the cabin."

Josh goes over to his saddle bag and pulls out what looks like a mobile phone from the dinosaur era.

"Yeah, doc, I'm gonna need you to get to the cabin. My girlfriend fell from the horse." He's silent for a minute before he speaks again. "No, the horse wasn't moving. She fell when she was dismounting."

I'm officially mortified. I get up and dust myself off. "I'm really fine, Josh. I don't need a doctor."

"We'll be there in an hour. I expect you to be ready by the time we make it back." Josh hangs up the phone.

"We need to get you back to see the doctor and make sure you are fine." His eyes travel up and down my body, more than once.

"Josh, trust me, it's just a scrape. Besides, I've had much worse than this before. I'll be fine."

"How do you know nothing's broken, Emmy? Shit, what if there's internal bleeding, or worse?"

"I've had broken bones before, Josh. I'd know if something were broken."

Shit, that was not the right thing to say, judging by the look on his face. "What broken bones have you had, Emmy? And how did you break them?"

I shake my head no. "You don't really want to know that, Josh. Let's not ruin the end of this trip."

Josh comes up to me, walking me into the tree. My back pressed up against it, he cages me in, one hand above my head with the other running through my hair. "What broken bones have you had, Emmy?"

"Uh, my arm?" It comes out as more of a question.

"Which arm? What else?"

"This one," I say, holding up my right arm.

"What else?"

"What else *what*?" Maybe I can use the dumb blonde card.

"What other bones have you had broken, Emmy?"

I don't miss his wording: not what bones have *I broken*, but what bones have I *had* broken.

I close my eyes. I can't see the look of disgust that's bound to happen when I tell him. "Ribs, mostly my ribs. A few fingers and toes. My arm—twice." I wince.

"Emmy, open your eyes," Josh whispers. I can feel his breath against my lips.

"Never again," he says as his mouth meets mine.

His kiss is quick, too quick. I need more.

"You're riding with me. Come on."

Josh picks me up, sitting me on top of Herbert before climbing up behind me. My hip is hurting like hell. But I don't say anything. It's nothing I can't handle.

He rides slowly back to the cabin, while guiding Cherry along next to us. I'm not going to lie—it's nice riding with Josh like this. I can feel him all around me, the warmth of his body mixed with the scent of his woodsy cologne surrounding me. By the time we make it back to the cabin, all I want to do is rip his clothes off and attack him.

"The doctor should be here by now," Josh says as we stop in front of the stables.

"I really don't need a doctor, Josh. You're overreacting. It's just a scrape."

"Humour me then, will you?" Josh says as he leads me into the cabin. The doctor is waiting in the living room. He stands up when he sees us.

"Mr. McKinley. Nice to see you, sir."

"Doc," Josh replies as he shakes his hand. "This is my girlfriend, Em—"

"Ember. And I really am fine. Josh is overreacting." I cut Josh off just as he's about to say my name. I didn't think about this. Fuck. Josh doesn't say anything, but he is sending me a very inquisitive look right now.

"*Ember* here fell off Cherry as she was dismounting. She landed on her left side." Josh looks right at me as he annunciates my alias.

"Okay, how about you take your jeans and shirt off and we'll have a look," the doctor says.

"Like fuck you will!" Josh yells. I grab his arm as he starts heading for the doctor.

"Sir, I need to be able to examine her." The doctor stands firm without backing away.

"You can do that with her clothes on her fucking body," Josh growls.

I, however, let go of Josh's arm, stand in front of him and strip my shirt over my head. Let's see how much he thinks I need a doctor now.

"What the fuck? Emmy, put that back on."

"You're the one who wanted the good doctor here to check me out, even though I'm fine. Well, now you have to deal with it. He's right. How's he supposed to see if anything's broken if I'm all covered up." I smile.

"Fuck, if I see one second of anything that I deem inappropriate, I will put a fucking bullet in your head, doc."

"No worries. I assure you I'm old enough to be Ember's grandfather. I'm also a professional, which is why you hired me in the first place."

"Okay, let's get this over with so you can go home, doctor. I'm so sorry Josh is wasting your time."

"Your wellbeing is far more important than anyone's time, Em." Josh sits down on the couch. His eyes do not leave the doctor's.

I undo my jeans and start pulling them down. I can't help the wince I let out when the denim rubs over my hip.

"Fuck, I knew something was wrong!" Josh is up and beside me like The damn Flash.

"I'm fine. It's just a little bruise."

"Stop, let me help." Josh removes my hands from my jeans and starts tugging them down. When I wince again, he stops and pulls a knife (one I didn't even know he had) from his ankle. Holding the denim as far away from my skin as he can, he slices it in half all the way down my left leg.

"Fucking Jesus, hell. Fuck. Em, that is not a fucking little bruise. Goddamn it," Josh curses and yells. He throws the knife behind me. I hear it hit a wall with a thud. I flinch and step away from him. I can't help it— it's instinctual.

He notices right away. "Emmy, I'm sorry. Sorry…" he says quietly as he slowly steps into me.

"Come, sit down—no, you should be on a bed. She should probably be in bed, right, doc?"

"Ah, let me have a look." The doctor bends down and lightly presses around my hip. For a bit, he's just prodding and poking.

"It's just some bruising. Apply ice twenty minutes on, ten minutes off, and rest. Don't go doing anything strenuous," the doctor finally says.

He packs all his equipment away before asking, "Mr. McKinley, can you walk me out?"

"Ah, yeah, sure." Josh picks up a throw and wraps it around me before sitting me on the couch. "I'll be back with an icepack. Don't move."

"Okay."

I know I said I wouldn't move, but after they leave the room, I follow anyway. I need to know what the doctor has to say. What if he recognised me?

Leaning against the wall, I catch bits of their hushed voices.

"Multiple wounds, scars," the doctor says.

"I'm aware," Josh grits out.

"I should be reporting this. It's ethical to report it. She's clearly in some type of trouble, Josh." Huh, he's calling him by his first name. They must be closer than they made it out to be.

"I appreciate your discretion, doc. I'm looking into it. Believe me when I say she *will* get her justice," Josh says.

I limp to the couch. I just get settled in when Josh comes back over. "You know, all you have to do is ask," he says.

"Ask what?"

"What the doctor had to say. I'd never lie to you, Emmy."

"Sorry…"

"Don't be. Here, hold this on your hip. I'm going to pack the car. Do you need anything else?" He hands me an icepack and a bottle of water.

"And take these," he instructs, handing me pills.

"What… what are they?" I ask warily. I don't like just taking random pills. Trent used to force me to take pills that would make me sleep for days. I had no control *or memory* of what he did with my body during those days. I'd wake up every now and then, wishing I hadn't.

"It's just Panadol, babe. Here." He pulls out a sheet of sealed pills, showing me the Panadol label. Rather than take the sealed sheet, I take the pills he already has out. This is Josh. I trust Josh. I swallow the pills before I can change my mind.

‾▽‾

THREE HOURS OF DRIVING, five hours of flying, and now we're almost at Josh's place. We're sitting in the back seat. Josh didn't want to drive so he had a car pick us up. I'm anxious as hell. I don't know what it is, but something is wrong. I can feel it in the pit of my stomach.

Josh is holding my hand, just like he always does in the car, his thumb absently twirling around my fingers.

"Josh, in case I didn't already tell you, I had a great time. I loved every minute with you. I love you, more than you'll ever know. Thank you for giving me this week," I tell him.

"Emmy, you don't need to thank me. There will be plenty more weeks like this in our future, babe." He smiles. I try to return the gesture, but it's fake. I know he can tell by the wrinkle in his eyes.

"What's wrong?" he asks as his phone rings. He takes it out of his pocket and looks at me. "Sorry, I have to take this." Squeezing my hand, he picks up the phone.

"What is it?"

I don't hear the other side of the conversation. But when Josh's eyes turn to me, I know it's not good.

"What's the name of the detective?" Josh asks into the phone. I wait, holding my breath.

"Detective Jones," Josh says, looking right at me. My body goes cold. I'm shaking. I can't stop the shaking. He's found me. How has he found me?

"Tell Detective Jones that I haven't seen Emily Livingston since high school. Last I heard, she died a few years back." Josh hangs up the phone. He tilts his head.

240

"John, change of plans. Take us back to the airport," he orders the driver before pressing a button and winding up the partitioner.

"Emily, care to explain why there is currently a Detective Jones at the farm with a warrant for your arrest?" Josh asks quietly.

He's too quiet. I can't tell if he's angry or not. I can't tell what he's thinking.

"I'm sorry. I'm so sorry. Just let me out here, Josh. You don't need to worry. I won't have you get into trouble because of me."

"You're not getting out of this fucking car, Emmy. I'm not letting you go. You need to tell me why there is a cop looking for you though. I can't help you if you don't talk to me."

"You can't help me, Josh. No one can…" I whisper.

"Whatever it is, Em, it can't be that bad. Just tell me, please."

"I-I killed him," I stumble out.

Josh doesn't even flinch, doesn't blink. His facial expression is blank. I just admitted to killing someone, and it's like I told him I wanted an ice cream cone or something.

"Who, Emmy? Who did you kill?" he urges.

"My husband."

Continue Josh and Emily's story in **Ruining Him, McKinley Ranch Duet, Book 2**

Josh

Emily came crashing back into my life, bringing with her everything I was missing.

But she's not the same girl I knew years ago. Gone is the girl who was always happy and eager to please everyone. The one who didn't let life get her down.

She's conquered her demons but they still haunt her whenever she closes her eyes. Her screams tear through the darkness night after night.

She thinks she needs to get away, to keep running. To leave me behind.

But I won't lose her again; I will slay anything, *anyone,* who thinks they can get in the way of my keeping her.

Emily

I wasn't meant to let myself get attached to Josh again. I wasn't meant to stay this long.

Now he knows my biggest secret; he knows I'm not the sweet girl he thinks I am.

I'm being chased, hunted down like prey.

But I won't let my past mistakes hurt Josh.

I need to leave before *he* finds me.

Leaving Josh behind is not going to be as easy as I thought it would be, but it's my only option. I'll do whatever it is I have to do to protect him, even if that means I have to **Ruin Him**.

Did you love the side characters? You can read all about the Merge world, through the series of standalone's and find out how all of the relationships play out!

Merged With Him (Zac and Alyssa's Story)
Fused With Him (Bray and Reilly's Story)
Entwined With Him (Dean and Ella's Story)
2nd Generation Merge Series
Ignited by Him (Ash and Breanna's Story)
An Entangled Christmas: A Merge Series Christmas Novel (Alex and Lily's Story)
Chased By Him (Chase & Hope's Story)
Tethered To Him (Noah & Ava's Story)

What's next after the McKinley Ranch Duet?
Read all about Holly and T's story in the Valentino Empire Trilogy.

Here's a little snippet from their beginning.

ACKNOWLEDGMENTS

I am thankful first to you, the reader, the one for whom this story was written. And I hope that you enjoyed Josh and Emily's story as much as I have.

Josh and Emily have taken me on an emotional rollercoaster. I cried, laughed and cursed them all in the same day. Their story truly touched my heart.

I am thankful for the support of my family. My wonderful husband, whose support and endless encouragement never fails. Nate, I could not have accomplished this without you.

I want to thank my beta readers. Natasha and Amy, you girls are one of a kind. Thank you for all of the time and effort you put into reading and providing insightful feedback for *Ruining Her*.

The Kylie Kent Street Team, what can I say? I would literally be nowhere if it weren't for you. I often get asked by other authors how I managed to form my street team. My answer is always the same, one hundred percent pure luck, and I'm not ever giving them back!! I believe I have the BEST street team in the business. Not only do you all ARC read for me, but you all read, promote and share whatever I put in front of you so enthusiastically and with genuine interest and excitement. I freaking love you guys!

Thank you, Kat, my amazing editor, who endures my constant messages and rants about these characters. Without you, this book would not be as great as it is now!

ABOUT THE AUTHOR

About Kylie Kent

Kylie made the leap from kindergarten teacher to romance author, living out her dream to deliver sexy, always and forever romances. She loves a happily ever after story with tons of built-in steam.

She currently resides in Sydney, Australia and when she is not dreaming up the latest romance, she can be found spending time with her three children and her husband of twenty years, her very own real life instant-love.

Kylie loves to hear from her readers; you can reach her at: author.kylie.kent@gmail.com

Let's stay in touch, come and hang out in my readers group on Facebook, and follow me on instagram.

Printed in Great Britain
by Amazon